Rise to Eminence

Rise to Eminence

by
Mark R. Sneller

Published by Fresh Air Press

Visit Mark's website at
marksneller.com

This edition was prepared for publication by
Ghost River Images
5350 East Fourth Street
Tucson, Arizona 85711
www.ghostriverimages.com

Cruise ship cover image from
Wikimedia Commons by permission
from Moonik

ISBN 978-1-7368917-3-5

Library of Congress Control Number: 2021924334

Printed in the United States of America
December, 2021

Other books Mark R. Sneller:

A Breath of Fresh Air

Greener Cleaner Indoor Air

Greener Cleaner Indoor Air – 2nd Edition

Toxic Exposure

Dying to Read

The Mars Virus Trilogy

    The Mars Virus

    The City Beneath the Earth

    Treasures

Strange Adventures

Contents

Cholera

One

In the heat of a summer's day, Jeff Shenero landed at Indira Gandhi International Airport in Delhi, India. The sights, sounds, smells, and smog of the capital city never ceased to saturate his senses, the scents of unfettered life. Red double-decker diesel-powered buses towered over sweaty rickshaw peddlers and pedestrians, as scooters wove through crowded intersections that had no signal lights. Civilization at its most raw form made one question the devil-may-care approach to life versus the values of higher civilization, bringing one's life into perspective. The concentration of over a billion people in a land mass only 40% that of the continental United States computed to five times the population density of the U.S.

Jeff had been there perhaps three years prior to explore and to visit his graduate student, Richard

Smith, who now taught full-time and did research at the University of New Delhi. Rick lived in a three bedroom home in an upscale portion of the city with neighbors from many international communities. He and his wife enjoyed a maid, cook, car, and driver, along with full medical care and good neighbors from a surprising number of nations. Not a bad life at all, for those willing to take the leap, Jeff thought. He had contemplated doing so himself on many occasions. He tried to call Richard to let him know he would be in town only to find out he had taken his family to Bangkok for two weeks.

This time Jeff was on the trail of a cholera outbreak in a fishing village on the east coast of the country, half-way between Calcutta to the north and Madras to the south. If Jeff had wanted to track the disease, he could have spent a lifetime doing so, as many had done and still do, from Haiti, to Africa, to Europe, to Southeast Asia. The occasional pinpoint flare-up of the disease in this isolated portion of the world caught his attention and pulled him like a magnet to find out why it hadn't spread. The disease was certainly communicable and caused by an intestinal bacterium associated with drinking contaminated water or eating contaminated food. It led to severe diarrhea and terrible dehydration, which led to death. It was generally associated with poverty, and/or catastrophic events. But why such a small scope to the problem, when typically, hundreds to thousands can be affected in a single outbreak.

After taking two days in Delhi to rest from the

24 hour flight from Oklahoma City, Jeff caught another flight southward to the Hyderabad airport in the southern Indian state of Andhra Pradesh. The progressive westernized city offered temptation for those who had limited cash, yet could live lavishly with the exchange rate of 20:1 rupees per dollar to enjoy all the amenities Richard Smith and family enjoyed in Delhi.

He needed to get to the seaport city of Visakhapatnam, or Visak, and take a bus to the fishing village associated in some manner with the outbreak, at least, according to the World Health Organization.

Upon arrival at the Hyderabad airport, Jeff inquired as to the location of the train station. An employee told him, "Just over there," pointing. Jeff should have remembered the old admonition: When in India, if you want directions to someplace, you ask three people. When two agree, you take the odd man out. Instead, he took one man's word and began walking *just over there*. "Oh, sir, in case you haven't heard, the railroad workers across the country are going on strike and the last train out will be leaving shortly."

Jeff had traveled the Indian trains before, from first class to third class unreserved. He was fully aware that Indian time was different than everybody else's time, but punctual habits are hard to break and he needed to hurry. He would have preferred to fly to Visak, but reportedly, a torrential monsoon rain had temporarily closed the airport, which meant he could pay a fortune to take a taxi, versus an inexpensive train, which would get him there about the same time.

He pulled out his collapsible sun hat and, preparing for the worst, began a fast walk. Thirty minutes later carrying a single suitcase and a full backpack, sweating through and through, Jeff checked his watch while dodging emaciated cattle, cars, buses, wandering dogs, bullock carts, scooters, countless people, and rickshaw drivers. Seeing no end to his efforts, he flagged down a rickshaw-walla peddling his bike and finally reached the station with five minutes to spare, only to find the train packed with people hanging onto the railing outside the car doors. Untold numbers others rode on top of the cars, willing to brave the miles to be traveled.

Jeff had read that the Indian rail system covered some 71,000 miles with over 7200 stops. Once pulled by coal burners, diesel and electric locomotives now dominated the rail system.

Looking at the poor souls desperate to reach their destination, he couldn't imagine subjecting himself to such torture, yet here were men who, from all appearances, were accustomed to such travel. The temperature would reach well over 100 degrees and with the train traveling at freeway speeds in this humidity, a wind-heat index could approach 130 degrees or above, yet here they were. He could think of some politicians he'd like to place on top of one of the trains so they might appreciate what they had.

Jeff walked the length of the concourse dodging

people, with the train to his right, looking for a place to get on, but finding none. He felt as though he were a meaningless dust mote among a million others until, at last, he found a uniformed conductor standing on the platform outside one of the cars. The man asked him for a ticket, which Jeff had neglected to purchase in his haste. He considered walking back to the station to buy the ticket, but he had no choice. He couldn't take a chance. There was no choice. He handed the conductor a ten dollar bill. The man took the money, but still stood in place and smiled, until Jeff handed him another ten. The conductor aggressively pushed others aside to enable Jeff to enter with his suitcase in his one hand and the bulky pack on his back. Both served as weapons to push others out of the way to permit his entry.

The train didn't leave for six hours. When it did, the ten-hour ride afterward became a nightmare with only a single bathroom per car. Occasional braless women dressed in cheap saris would shove through the packed mass of sweating and overheated humanity while smoking a stubby cigar. When they reached the door to the bath, they would take the cigar from their mouth, reverse it, enter the bath, and after coming out, would reposition the cigar with the lit end outward again. Jeff later learned that the people who did this had the highest rate of oral cancer in the world. No surprise there.

Jeff had learned to keep his credit cards and IDs in his left front pocket and his cash and cell phone in his right front pocket, to eliminate the possibility of a rising entrepreneur razor-cutting his back pocket to extract the wallet of a Westerner. He also learned to use a wide, comfortable, elastic bandage to connect his right wrist to his suitcase. On this lengthy journey, he brought his backpack to his chest to protect its contents.

Over the hours, the train made a number of stops. When it did pull into a station, passengers on the top of the train and within it found a way to readjust or depart. On one such occasion, Jeff worked his way into a newly vacated seat, his suitcase jamming the area between his seat and the one in front of him and his backpack clutched to his front. Around his neck, he wore a man-purse in which he carried his passport, secondary IDs, chargers, and a loaded electronic book. He'd never touch one at home, but on the road it served as a wonderful tool for limitless games and books to read, access to Google's data base of the world's knowledge, GPS, and weighed only ounces. The best part: One never ran out of reading material and things to do with it.

At one stop, he chanced to look out the window to see a thermometer reading 101 degrees. His sports watch read 1:27 am.

Over time, the journey brought Jeff to the port city of Visak in the middle of another exceedingly hot and humid day. Hiring a taxi to take him to his hotel, Jeff took a shower, changed clothes, ate a good dinner, drank a quart of beer—the smallest quantity available—and watched a soap opera on TV. Beyond tired, he had no difficulty sleeping in the bed housed beneath mosquito netting with a noisy fan overhead.

In the morning, his several days of travel from home neared its end, with only a short bus ride left to the village. Jeff looked out the window of his fourth floor suite, newly rebuilt after a devastating hurricane had struck the port city only a few years before. Finally feeling relaxed, Jeff worked in a half-hour of calisthenics, dressed, ate a light breakfast of eggs, toast, and coffee, and took a short time to explore the various stores. He had no idea where he would stay in the village of his destination. His research online had borne no fruit in that regard. He thought he might take a bus there to make initial inquiries, and return to the hotel the same day.

The hotel was situated in the middle of a long thoroughfare in a city of some 20 million. Along both sides of the wide dirt boulevard, Jeff passed fruit and vegetable stores. He passed cigarette stands selling single cigarettes for those in immediate need. He passed clothing and hardware stores, most with awnings to keep out heat and rain.

In some strange regard, Jeff felt totally comfortable in these surroundings. Call it eugenics, call it racial memory, call it what it you will, Jeff felt at home, yet always wary in any new environment.

Within several minutes, he found a small book store not much larger than a bedroom with the heavily bearded proprietor seated and reading at a small front desk. The man stood at Jeff's entrance. "Welcome, my name is Raj Singh, you can call me Raj. Please let me know if I can help you with anything," offered the turbaned Sikh in perfectly accented British English. Immediately, Jeff thought the man's family probably originated in the northern state of Punjab, a state that bragged noteworthy politicians, businessmen and fighters. Now the man operated a small book store. India was indeed a land of curiosities.

Two

After their ninety-year occupation of India, the British left behind several important contributions: a system of government, the English language, a postal service, and the railroad—completely converted to diesel and electric powered. Although virtually all of the 28 states had their own language replete with its own script, English was commonly spoken among the middle and upper classes, and commonly taught in schools. In fact, students spent a significant amount of time, not only learning English, but also the language of their state and the adjoining state(s), as well as Hindi, in many cases. This limited the time spent on other subjects, yet the country managed to turn out a high percentage of intellectuals and top-level scientists.

Jeff turned to the man and replied, "Yes, thank you, I'm sure I will. My name is Jeff."

"Ah, an American. Please look around and ask if you have any questions," said Raj, obviously astute as to the nuances between the languages.

In front of Jeff were three walls of mostly hard-cover books. Enveloped by a cloak of knowledge, he became immediately attracted to a massive tome on the oceans located on a shelf labeled Earth Sciences. Pulling out the book, he noted the pages were extremely thin, almost like onion skin, but well printed. He walked it over to Raj to ask him about the printing. He had never seen anything like it before.

"Yes, these books are all copied and reprinted in China and sold to us for pennies on the dollar. The price is $7.50 for you instead of $95 you would pay for it in the States."

Surprised at the answer, Jeff returned the book to the shelf and browsed through the philosophy section, keeping a wary eye on the time. Randomly scanning the books he found himself dumbfounded reading titles of such outliers as *The Neurophysiological Basis of Mind by* Eccles, *The Philosophy of Time, The Physics of Throwing a Baseball*, and Huxley's *Brave New World.*

He picked up another titled *Pictorial Guide to the Seashells of India* by Grace Chatfield, impressed by the detailed descriptions and the colored photographs. Turning to the Microbiology section, he saw his own book *Medical Aspects of the Fungi,* by Jeffrey Shenero, Ph.D. In a strange way, he felt honored the Chinese would chose to steal his copyrighted book.

He decided to purchase it for the rupee equivalent of an even $4.75 when his students paid some fifteen times that amount. Those who didn't want to pay the money could probably find it online for free, after a little stealthful browsing.

Jeff also bought the seashell book and, placing them in his stripped-down back pack, returned to the shelves.

A short while later, another man walked into the store and greeted Raj. The man had a British accent. He heard Raj say an American was in the store, at which time the man approached Jeff. Dressed in summer white and wearing a white, broad- brimmed sun hat, the man greeted Jeff, "Hallo, chap, my name is Henry James. You are the American?"

Jeff turned to see the inquisitor in his sixties, clean cut, three inches shorter than himself, with a slight paunch and jovial smile.

"No, not that Henry James," admitted the Brit.

Jeff found the man to be compelling, very open, and obviously willing to chat. The men engaged in small talk for some time, feeling out one another, when the Brit announced, "Say, old boy, are you ready for lunch. I'm feeling like Chinese food at the wharf."

Jeff checked his watch. He supposed another day wouldn't matter.

"Going someplace?" Henry asked.

Jeff shrugged it off. "At some point I need to get to Bhiminipatnam."

"Bimli? Why, I live there," declared Henry, jovially. Jeff half-expected a slap on the back. "I'll drive you there after lunch, if you like. My treat."

Jeff acceded to the request for lunch and the men began to leave the open front of the store. As they did so, Raj said, "Henry, and Jeff, is it? Why don't you both come to my house this evening and have dinner with us, if you're up to another visit, Henry."

Henry looked at Jeff, who thought for an instant, then nodded. Henry said, "Absolutely, we'll see you at 9:00."

Raj said to Jeff, "Say, do I know you?"

Jeff smiled, "Not unless you go to Norman, Oklahoma, a lot."

Raj cocked his head slightly. Pulling out his cell he began to make a call, while the two men waved down a couple of rickshaw drivers in a sea of traffic. They were driven to the restaurant designated by Henry. It stood on the wharf overlooking the Bay of Bengal where numerous ships lay at anchor. Seagulls floated, or landed on posts, while cormorants dive-bombed for fish. The air was breezeless and heavy with moisture. The pair found a table for two with merchant seamen occupying the larger tables, some speaking Japanese, others Greek, and still others Italian. Plates and bowls of Chinese foods of every ilk were being passed around.

Henry ordered beer and food for them both and explained, "I've known Raj for a number of years. He's one of six sons. His father is a federal judge. One brother is a scientist, another a lawyer, another a doctor, another an inventor, another a pilot, and Raj doubles as district magistrate. Twice a month he and his driver take the 4-wheel-drive Jeep Cherokee into the jungle to visit the different tribes to see if they needed anything. He'll have the back loaded with goodies, mostly foodstuffs and medical supplies. I've gone with him. You should too. It's quite an interesting ride. We got stuck in a mud hole once during a terrible rainstorm and had to get out and push to escape. He told me to always be prepared for the unexpected out there."

A surge of excitement swept through Jeff. There it was, without him having to search around for a way to get into the jungles, the second reason for his coming to India. He stored the information.

Jeff felt comfortable enough with Henry to ask, "I'm curious about you. I mean, why do you live in a fishing village? What are you doing here?" He waved his hand around.

Harry laughed, pulled out a handkerchief from somewhere and took off his hat to wipe his forehead and temples beneath a mop of gray hair. "Me? I made my money by buying a single motel and developing a nationwide chain of motels both in the States and in Britain. A number of years ago, a good friend of mine named Chatfield came to know Raj's father, the judge, on a business trip here and said he was looking for place off the beaten path to retire. The judge introduced Chatfield to Raj, who found him a decent house in Bimli, so he recommended it to me and my wife. She passed a few years ago.

"Bye the bye, if you've heard of Chatfield pharmaceuticals, well, that's him. As for me, when at home, I play tennis and cards with retired Indians and occasionally fish. Every two or three weeks I come here into the big city to eat well and go to the theater. Are you looking to retire there, as well?"

"Not at all, I'm going there to follow the cholera crisis," Jeff announced.

Harry narrowed his eyes and looked at Jeff somewhat askance, "What crisis? I don't know anything about it?"

Jeff shook his head in confusion. "The WHO reported it. I'm a scientist and an investigator of sorts. How can you not know about an epidemic in your own village, or maybe it's one close to yours. WHO didn't exactly specify, only that it may have stemmed from the Bimli area."

The food and beer arrived, along with two glasses of water. "Don't drink the water, just to be safe," Henry cautioned. Using chopsticks, the men ate in silence for some time until Henry said, "Look, old boy, tell me where you're staying and I'll pick you up around 8:30 this evening. After Raj's party, I'll bring you back and I'll go to my own hotel. In the morning I'll drive you to my little village and you can see for yourself all is well. In fact, I'll introduce you to some friends and to the local chieftain. No doubt, he'll welcome you as an honored guest and use your visit as an excuse to have a party, drinks included. Rumor has it a new shipment of Johnny Walker came in."

Three

At first glance, Raj's colorless two-story home seemed to be built of concrete and stucco. When the two men arrived in Henry's standard Tata

Motor's black sedan, they found a number of other similar cars parked in front, along with a two BMW convertibles and a Cadillac Escalade.

"Looks like we lucked out, Henry, and got invited to a big party. No cheap dates here," Jeff said.

Henry smiled. Jeff didn't get it.

Raj met the pair at the door at the door and let them into a sitting room where a good dozen men awaited their arrival, including Raj's father, a tall handsome man, also bearded, whose turban gave him even greater height. The women remained in the kitchen and dining area, completing preparations for the feast and setting the large dinner table. They would eat later. A large jar of mentholated cream stood on a lone table in a hallway beneath a mirror, where men would occasionally unscrew the cap, inhale from the contents, replace the cap, and move on. "Clears the sinuses," Henry said, in answer to Jeff's unasked question.

Jeff felt emotional warmth within the home well decorated with expensive furnishings and paintings, similar to homes of the wealthy around the globe, a complete turnaround from the sterile appearing exterior.

Out of politeness, none of the guests directly mentioned what Raj had told them about Jeff, but during the conversation, Raj innocently asked Jeff what he did for a living. One of the brothers—the scientist—announced, "Yes, you're the one who stopped the terrorist threat in the States not long ago. You even received a presidential award for it."

The others, already advised by Raj as to Jeff's identity, began to recall what they had heard, some of it exaggerated and not all of it true. Jeff soon found himself fawned over, forced to tell the story in some detail until a senior staff woman announced dinner was served. In his naiveté, Jeff finally realized the truth. Raj had set up the party for him.

Half of those at the table ate the various dishes with their right hand only, others used utensils. Several of the dishes were so hot as equal the most spicy on the planet. Jeff's head and armpits sweat freely. Before him stood dishes of beef and vegetable curries with lentils, rice, tandoori chicken, lamb, and Nan.

Once the judge had ensured Jeff had consumed enough refills to prevent starvation, he requested deserts to be served. At last the judge leaned over to Jeff, who suffered from a severe case of bloating and overeating, saying, quietly, "They're waiting for you to burp."

"Thank you," Jeff whispered in return, letting go over an hour's worth of pent up energy, at which time everyone sighed in relief knowing their guest had enjoyed the meal.

"Shall we adjourn?" the judge declared, making a move to stand. Jeff noted with some interest that half the buttons on the man's shirt were broken, a sure indication someone laundered his clothing by rubbing it with bar soap and beating it against rocks or a concrete basin to loosen the dirt, the standard cleaning practice.

Everyone arose at once and moved to the smoking room where a few drinks were poured and smokers lit up either cigars or cigarettes. The scientist brought out a beedi, a small, thin, inexpensive cigarette manufactured by the billions and composed of flaked tobacco wrapped in a *tendu* tree leaf and tied at one end. It contained only a trace of nicotine with the leaf decomposing into carbon dioxide and water, as opposed to toxic phenolic compounds, carcinogenic unto themselves, which are produced by the burning of cigarette paper.

After only a minute, Harry announced "Jeff came here from America because he heard there is a cholera outbreak in Bimli. Isn't that right, Jeff?"

"Absolutely," Jeff admitted. "I try to track these things and sometimes they're linked to odd events, such as volcanic explosions and odd weather patterns. It is also well known to be associated with algal and phytoplankton bloom here and in South America. What can anyone tell me about this outbreak? Harry claims ignorance of the problem."

The large group of men looked at one another, a clear sign no one had knowledge of the issue. The doctor said, "I do see occasional incidences of cholera associated with hurricanes, even as recently as four years ago when we were devastated. Sanitation became poor; well, poorer than it is now, but none have occurred in the local region to match what you describe."

Becoming drowsy and eager to get on with his investigation, Jeff felt a sense of relief when the long get-together had ended Harry drove him back to his hotel.

Unlike the previous evening's sleep when he had passed out from fatigue, this night he slept poorly, if at all. He suffered from gastric upset combined with a fan hangover. He had defined the clinical condition years before during his travels when a fan blew onto his head throughout the night to drive the mosquitoes away, and the noise of its motor kept him awake. After he turned it off and returned to bed, he soon heard mosquitoes cavorting outside the net, some with high pitch whines and some with lower pitched whines. sometimes one immediately following the other, as though racing past the net near his face trying to sneak a peek at their prey before mating.

Something Henry had said earlier popped into Jeff's mind in the middle of the night and he definitely wanted to pursue it. In the morning, he asked Henry to contact Raj to find out when he planned to make his next trip into the jungle and could Jeff come along to collect various species of unidentified fungi. Jeff already had the permits, mini-freeze packs to keep samples cold for 36 hours, a small, but complete, medical kit, and he had researched the vipers, cobras, kraits, and poisonous plant species he might encounter.

Henry made the call and to Jeff's pleasant surprise, Raj said he would be leaving in two mornings for the day and he would be honored to have Jeff along for the ride.

Jeff and Harry stood at the open door entrance to Harry's beachfront home to look at the bay where numerous fishing boats were operated by dark-skin natives, each holding four to six men who worked the nets. Dark clouds loomed on the eastern horizon. Whether it rained or not remained to be seen. By late afternoon the boats would bring in a haul of grouper, snapper, tuna, and an occasional smaller shark. These were gutted, cleaned, and sold on the market the next day. Bimli's single, but large, ice machine, located in the post office, served to provide enough cubes each day to preserve the catch, with the postal workers getting their fair share of returns in exchange.

A few crabs had left the sanctity of the sand to find the concrete flooring of the home an interesting surface upon which they might scuttle. The home had been constructed almost a century earlier by the British and occupied some 3000 square of feet of cement flooring with two great rooms, a small kitchen and dining area, and a single room large enough to sleep ten. The commode and shower were located in a separate building to the north. Showers could be obtained by ladling cold well-water from a large bucket to be poured over one's body, unless one chose to place heating coil into a bucket of water for a special treat of warm water.

"You'll like the people, natives and otherwise. They're quite welcoming," Harry offered.

Jeff nodded, "That's been my experience wherever I travel. It's the nature of people, as long as the government stays out of their lives."

"Here, here," Harry assented. "Are you ready for a little walk down the beach? I want to introduce you to the local chief. He's elderly, but enjoys a good laugh. He doesn't speak English, but I speak Telugu and Hindi. I'll introduce you."

Harry led Jeff down a path past an old 17th Century walled-in Dutch graveyard, then to the shoreline itself, only 100 yards away. They turned south to walk perhaps a half-mile where they encountered several loin-clothed natives debarking their small fishing boat, hauling it onto the land with a pile of fish still in the boat. One thin young man ten years of age stood atop a huge sea turtle that had crawled onto the sand to lay its eggs.

Harry greeted the men, one of whom asked whether Jeff would trade his camera for the man's loincloth. Jeff politely declined the offer but handed the man a five rupee note for his kind offer, and the westerners walked on for another few minutes until turning abruptly westward into the foliage. Within seconds, they found themselves amidst a number of huts, mostly vacated by men at the moment, their occupants out on the seas.

Huts stood some distance from the water amidst palm trees and local vegetation. Numerous animals walked about at random including pigs, chickens, cattle, goats, water buffaloes, an occasional peacock, as well as domestic animals. Fighting cocks cackled beneath large overturned baskets made of woven palm fronds.

Jeff saw an elderly man on a rocking chair on the packed earth in what appeared to be a broad circle of huts surrounding the one the men headed toward. The tribal chieftain grinned when he saw Henry, who came over to introduce Jeff as his American friend. The chief stood, looked Jeff over up and down. Touching his skin and bald head, he said something to Henry, who laughed.

"He said 'A real American. "Now he's seen it all,'" Henry remarked

Jeff said, "Tell him I'm from Hollywood."

"Are you?"

Jeff replied, "No, I'm from Oklahoma, but we might get some perks, if you tell him a stretch. I did go through there once."

Henry laughed and did as Jeff requested.

Obviously impressed, the chief asked if he had been in any movies, Jeff considered this. Movies were huge in India, a country that probably produced more per year than almost any other country, including the United States and China. Its term for the industry was Bollywood. Because the chieftain hadn't specified the type of movie, Jeff told him he had been in several. He failed to mention they were home videos, of which the man would likely have no knowledge, anyway.

The chief slapped his leg and told Henry, "We will have a celebration tonight. A shipment of Jack Daniels came in," and pointed to a crate to his right.

Henry had already heard about it the day before from one of the fishermen, but said nothing.

Henry and Jeff ate a very light early dinner of soup and bread at Henry's house to arrive at the party well after dark, which seemed to be a standard time for eating. A bonfire greeted them with men sitting in a circle around it drinking rice beer served by braless women wearing loose saris. The case of liquor remained unopened.

Upon the arrival of the guests of honor, the chief asked everyone to stand and applaud, went to the case, opened it, pulled out a bottle, took a drink, and set it next to his chair. He took another, passed it to Jeff, who took a swallow, and passed it to Henry. The chief took out more bottles to make the rounds. Curiously, the men only drank half of each bottle as the evening wore on, then one of them returned it to the case.

A cauldron of hot soup stood over on a fire pit. Women ladled out the thick fish and vegetable soup into wooden bowls for each man who drank from the bowl directly or used a wooden spoon. Marveling at the flavor, albeit spicy, Jeff asked Henry about the unrecognizable pieces in the soup.

"Sea turtle," Henry replied.

After each man had downed several bowls of soup and had consumed a sufficient amount of whiskey, the dancing and singing began which lasted well into the night. The affair ended abruptly when the chief declared it so, curiously at the same time the liquor ran out. In any case, the sun would rise soon and the boats must go out at dawn.

The two men fairly staggered along the beach

back to the house, using the flashlights on their cells to help them avoid occasional rocks. At 2:00 am, Jeff's cell phone vibrated in his hand. He didn't expect any calls down here in Bimli, although the distance was well within the range of the towers in Visak. Ignoring it, he asked a question that had been burning his tongue all evening. "Where did they get the booze from?"

"Come on, old chap, there's a seaport only twenty miles up the coast, the one where we met. This is Raj's district and when he can, he likes to keep his people happy."

"But why do they only drink only half the bottle?" Jeff inquired, completely stumped by the practice.

"Ah, yes. Well, they fill the other half with USDA pesticide, then and send it up the coast to another village. When the others get sick, our chief claims his people took a little out of each bottle and had no trouble at all and can't understand why anybody would get ill. It's not Raj's concern, because the other village is out of his district. Not knowing what happened, the other chief is up against it with his own people and has to tell his own district supervisor that cholera hit many of his people. The supervisor must report a cholera incident to the World Health Organization. No big deal. It's politics between tribes, as usual. When you first inquired, I thought you meant a real epidemic and I didn't think of this until now."

"Wait a minute. Why didn't our guys just drink it all and be done with it?" Jeff slurred, trying to wrap his head around what he had learned.

Henry shrugged. "Our chief likes to maintain good relations with his neighbors. Besides, he doesn't believe what he added to the whiskey will hurt anyone. Okay, it tastes bad by itself, but when blended with alcohol, hell, it wouldn't hurt a fly."

Jeff struggled with trying to apply his intellect to the thought process of a fishing village chief and couldn't make it work.

At least the issue of the cholera outbreak had been resolved, even if it cost him a couple of thousand dollars for a trip around the world for two nights of partying.

He decided against lamenting about time and money spent on this investigation and focused on flopping onto his bed, turning on the mosquito fan, and was on the verge of passing out when his phone vibrated again. He would return the call when he damn well felt like it.

Pigeons and the Orange Mold

Before noon of the same day, Jeff sat by the open doorway of Henry's house within the screened-in front porch measuring some six-feet by thirty-feet. With electronic book in hand, he looked out at the turbulent waters of the bay through a torrential downpour. According the Henry, the landscape of the bay would completely rearrange with the appearance and disappearance of sand bars and rip tides.

A standing fan served to blow the heavy moist air from his skin, his head hurting from the recent debauchery. Harry had been out somewhere when he suddenly appeared with a man and woman in tow, all three wearing sandals and holding large black umbrellas.

"Jeffrey, old chap, I'd like you to meet two friends of mine I was telling you about, Steven and Grace Chatfield. They're also from across the pond," Harry announced.

The man was lean, clean shaven, and stood over six feet in height with gray hair sparse over the ears and bald on top. He appeared to be comfortable with himself and in his mid-to-late sixties. The woman was short, well kept, with a cheerful countenance wearing a sun hat with no makeup. Both were dressed in loose shirts and shorts, befitting the season. Steven identified himself as a retired pharmaceutical executive who had traveled the world with his wife, had been to the States on a number of occasions, and had certainly heard of the famous Dr. Shenero. Out of modesty, he failed to mention his father had founded Chatfield Pharmaceuticals a century ago, a multi-billion dollar corporation, and had turned over the company to his son, Steven, who had retired in turn, because his own son had become CEO.

Jeff remembered the book on seashells he had purchased and mentioned it to Grace. "Yes, it's my book. It took me years to put it together. I'm not certain I've earned back my money. It's not exactly flying off the shelves," she cheerily announced.

Harry led the trio inside where he ordered his servant to prepare tea and cookies while the four sat at the dining room table. A very large screened window looked out over a hand-smoothed clay tennis court in the backyard where the water ran off in different directions.

Several minutes of polite discussion passed when Steven asked, "Jeffrey, I'm wondering if you can help us with something. We need some fresh ideas."

"Of course, if I can," Jeff replied.

Grace said, "We have something running around in our attic, mostly at night. We can't figure out how it gets up there or goes in and out. Sometimes, it sounds like its fighting with another creature. We haven't been able to get a good night's sleep in a long time.

Jeff frowned. "Do you have any exterior holes to the attic?"

"Only bird holes for ventilation, and they're screened in," Grace contributed.

"I'll take a look at it, but no guarantees," Jeff offered, puzzled about how he could possibly help the couple.

Steven said, "Tell you what. If you fix the problem for us . . . how are you getting home?"

"What? Oh, flying," Jeff shook his head, confused by the question.

"Good. You give me your tickets and we'll change them all to first class. We'll pay for it all."

Jeff laughed out loud, definitely not taking the offer seriously. "Okay, but only if I can fix the problem. How about today, if the rain ever lets up?"

Three hours later, Harry led Jeff to the Chatfield residence only a quarter-mile up the hill. They crossed the main thoroughfare of the village with a population of perhaps 8,000, although only a few hundred might be seen at once at the various stands lining both sides of a single dirt road. A bus stop was situated at the end of the street next to a hotel, or hottle, a name reserved for a small café.

The single story home appeared as any other with

a heavy red clay shingle roof and a concrete porch resembling the one in front of Harry's house. Jeff asked Steven about the purpose of ledge beneath the bird holes.

Steven replied, "It's decorative."

"Makes no sense," Jeff said.

"Have you ever been to a country where everything makes sense?" Steven asked.

"Got me there," Jeff replied.

"Pigeons roost there and even make nests. It's quite a mess," Grace inserted.

Jeff said, "No big deal. You can get somebody to clean the ledge. I see the bird holes are screened over so your critter can't be going in through them."

Steven pointed, "The portion you're looking at got repaired a couple of months ago during the dry season after we had leakage problems. It stayed open for a couple of weeks."

Jeff rubbed his chin. "Hmmm, I have an idea. Do you have a ladder?"

Steven left and soon returned with a stepladder. Jeff climbed up and noted the piles of pigeon droppings on the entire length of the ledge. He pushed on the screen of one of the bird holes and it held. He did so on a second with the same result. The third one easily folded inward, hinged by wire on the inside at the top.

Jeff climbed down the latter to face the others and said, "Here's my theory. Your friend doesn't go in an out because he can't go out. He lives in there and probably got in during construction.

"Any pigeon pushing against the screen goes right into the attic space, but can't get out again because the wire only goes one way. Your little attic friend is happy to have the company and the food after it wins the fights you're hearing. You can set up vertical spikes around the ledge or a roll of wire, if you don't care what it looks like to keep off the pigeons and your friend won't last long without food."

The husband and wife looked at each other and smiled. Grace said, "We'll make sure to reinforce the screen and check the security of the others so more two or four legged creatures can't get in there."

About to reply, Jeff's phone vibrated once more. This time, almost automatically, he pulled it out of his pocket and checked the screen. The call came from Carmen, his sweetheart. That must have been her on the previous occasions. He'd forgotten to return her calls. Something was going on.

He held up a finger to the others and walked away several yards to answer the call.

"Hi, honey," he said, innocently.

"Why didn't you call me back?" Carmen asked.

"Sorry, it was 2:00 in the morning here and we were coming back from . . . a get-together."

"I'm happy for you," Carmen said, with obvious concern. "Well, our lives have been threatened and I'm scared, but I guess you were too busy to call me back."

A wash of guilt swept over Jeff, quickly recalling the dinner with Raj's family, getting hammered at the party with the fishermen, and now chasing a rat, or whatever, in somebody's attic.

"How so?" Jeff inquired.

"Threating calls on our home and business lines that say we're both going to pay for what you've done," Carmen asserted.

"Done what?" Jeff asked.

"They don't say," Carmen summarized.

"Oh, boy. Honey, I'll wrap things up here and come home as soon as I can. I'll let you know my schedule as soon as I find out." Jeff replied. It hurt him to see her flustered like this. Why would anybody threaten him? On the other hand, why wouldn't they? He had plenty of enemies. Painfully, Jeff would have to decline Raj's offer to go on a jungle ride and returned to his new friends to ask a big favor.

On the short walk back to the house, he noticed a pile of rubble to one side comprised of roofing tiles, tar paper, and a few pieces of lumber. Patches of orange on the tar paper caught his attention and he moved in for a closer look. Pulling out his cell phone, he opened the magnifier app and zoomed in for a 30x magnification. The orange patches were growths of some kind. He took several photos and turned to his friends, asking about the pile.

Grace said, "Leftovers from the roof repair. They were supposed to take it away a long time ago."

"Mind if I take a sample of this with me?" Jeff inquired.

Steven laughed. "Jeffrey, you can take the whole damn pile, if you want."

Poison in the Mail

One

Jeff not only flew first class, but flew head of the class, getting bumped in seating and in flights ahead of others. After telling his friends what Carmen had said, in exchange for the favor, he promised to let them know about events happening at home, as soon as he found out himself.

The long journey gave Jeff a chance to catch up on sleep with a lot of time to think. He needed more information from Carmen, of course, but he felt confident the threat had nothing to do with his research institute. A lot of big people got sent to prison because of the terrorist plot he had unraveled, which opened up endless possibilities. The president, his senator, and the FBI would likely become involved. On the other hand, his gut told him it might be tied to one of the countless in-home jobs he had conducted. Would he have to go through all of his years of job notes?

Some 30 hours later, Carmen picked him up at Will Rogers International Airport at OKC and drove down to their home in Norman, a short 40 minute drive. On the way she explained about the calls to his medical institute and at home, a single male voice making the simple statement. Both of them are going to be destroyed for what he had done and they need to start looking over their shoulders. The calls could be traced to a burner phone. The caller had the slightest of foreign accents and it wasn't Spanish. With the trace of a rolled "R", the caller could be from almost anywhere outside the U.S.

At home, Jeff copied the recording onto his phone's memory, then they drove to his institute where he did the same thing. Before leaving, the couple found some carton boxes and loaded into them the past five years of his record books, those records prior to his involvement in the terrorist plot and his subsequent startup of the research center.

Unless tied to the plot, still a strong possibility, Jeff wondered why anybody would wait years to come after him. For the next several hours, the couple paged through his house-call jobs where he inspected for mold, took air samples to check for general air quality, collected surface and wall cavity samples, came back to the lab to check them under the microscope, write the report, and email or snail-mail the bill along with it.

After sending out for pizza, the evening turned out to be surprisingly interesting, as each recounted a particular case that drew their interest, occasionally causing laughter.

Carmen remembered the case where Jeff monitored a single-wide mobile home. The wife sold real estate and the husband worked construction. Upon marriage years before, the husband had ordered her never to enter the second bathroom. He declared the bath to be his alone. When Jeff had entered, he found it so disgusting that he almost vomited and decided against telling the wife what he had discovered to save their marriage.

Jeff began to chuckle while he reviewed the Doug Johnson notes, remembering the case. He had been called to inspect a better home where the wife suspected mold might be present due to an under-sink water leak. He found the husband at home with the wife at work. During the course of his testing, Doug said, "Say, Jeff, do you drink?"

"Not much," Jeff answered. "As a matter of fact, I'm thinking of quitting all together."

"Oh, too bad," Doug said.

"Why too bad?" Jeff asked, curiously.

"Well, last night my wife and I threw a big blowout party, the last hurrah. We had promised each other we would never drink again and would support each other though our efforts as we went through life."

"I'm impressed with your strength of resolve," Jeff told him.

Doug continued, "We also said we'd give any liquor we had left over to the first person who came along, which would be you."

This stopped Jeff in his tracks and like a good politician, quickly back tracked.

"Well, I said I was thinking about quitting. I mean, it wouldn't be all at once, anyway. It would be a phased approach. Why, what do you have left over?"

"This way," Doug said, and led Jeff to the garage where shelves were lined with bottles, like a liquor store. Some bottles were small, others large, some half empty, others unopened.

"You can have them all if you want," offered Doug.

Fifteen minutes later, at 11:00 am, Jeff drove off with four large boxes filled with liquor bottles and a check in his pocket. Carmen took two bottles white wine, he took a bottle of Patron Tequila, and gave the rest to friends. He became their hero.

When Jeff read about the case where a retired policeman had hired Jeff, his internal alarm bells rang. The job occurred some seven years earlier and involved a situation he soon forgot about after it had closed. Real life intervened and his mind had turned elsewhere.

The simple four-page report had turned into 10,000 pages on the man's background. The case came back to him in a rush. A policeman in Alabama had been fired by the department for numerous instances of abusive behavior and he found another job as a repairman in Seattle, before moving to Oklahoma City.

"Right," Jeff said, leaning back in his chair, remembering, thinking about the threatening calls. "A couple of months later, this guy, Abbot, a renter, filed a million dollar suit against me, the management company, and the home owners. He complained both he and his wife and their two year old son had of a variety of symptoms. Many of the symptoms were remarkably ingenious."

Carmen completed the picture. "Abbot got sent to prison for five years, not for filing a bogus claim, but because you found him engaged in illicit arms trading and he needed money to pay off a debt."

"Let me make a call to the attorney who represented us," Jeff offered.

Some twenty minutes later, he found out Abbot had been released from prison only four weeks prior to the threatening calls and regularly checked in with his parole officer.

"What are we going to do?" Carmen asked, clearly frightened.

Jeff said, almost too casually to suit Carmen, "I'm not worried about the house. Between the security system and the Rottweilers, we should be all right there. Keep in mind, bad guys are looking for Abbot, too, because he still owes them. I'm sure he has problems of this own. Anyway, let's get ahold of Sheriff Parker."

Jeff had a disconcerting thought. Focusing his attention on the obvious might be the wrong approach. He might be missing the real problem.

Two

No further threatening calls came in over the next several days during which time Jeff and Carmen continued to review his old records. They tried to spin each one into a criminal conspiracy where danger to them might be involved, but could come up with nothing other than a few chuckles. The time-delay factor served to be a major issue: Typically, a person isn't threatened for something wrong they'd done years before.

Abbot remained at a half-way house under observation and thus far had exhibited no untoward behavior. The house limited use of the phone, which meant little when burners were as common as contraband drugs.

When the third threat came in, voice analysis found it to be identical to the first two. In fact, all three were playbacks of a recording with no possibility of tracing the call.

Jeff and Carmen had no choice but to continue to work as though nothing had happened, although they kept a wary eye taking care to vet any person wishing to come to the research center for any manner of business.

Jeff maintained a full-time staff of eight with another three graduate students, thanks to a generous government grant. After uncovering the plot by the terrorists to poison the ink of newspapers and add the toxin toothpaste and face cream, the government believed Jeff to be the best man to analyze and clear hundreds of products in the consumer marketplace.

Now, with his own laboratory paid for by the feds, Jeff retired from his professorship at the University of Oklahoma and occasionally traveled the world looking for new species of fungi possessing antimicrobial properties.

Within a short time, after the bloom had worn off the rose, his workers became disgruntled. They were top of the line researchers recruited from around the world who were relegated to performing menial tasks that college graduate students could do. Self-satisfaction doesn't come from receiving a lot of money for a job you're not happy with.

A knock at the door brought the couple out of their page turning. Emily Harrison opened the door. Diminutive, wearing her white lab coat, with spiked black hair and glasses, she was one of Jeff's brainiac doctoral candidates who played first chair violin for the Oklahoma Symphony Orchestra, when she could get away. She specialized in using fungal toxins as antibiotics in combination with other antibiotics, the same as Jeff's. She was one of those people who are easy to dislike because they don't have any evident faults and are successful in everything they attempt.

"Yes, Emily," Jeff said.

"Doctor, the orange sample you gave me won't grow in culture unless I add a little mineral oil. I can't figure out where the heck it might grow in nature. After I added the oil. I grew a batch of it in liquid culture in only three days instead of the normal two to three weeks. It's a nice orange flat mat with no spores. On Petri plates it creates a clear zone of inhibition around it. Nothing can get close. So it's excreting a powerful toxin."

This brought to mind a study Jeff had read debunking the notion that some molds produce toxins to inhibit competition. Researchers found this to be a false assumption. They found no genetic code could be found associated with toxin production, thus it is not a survival mechanism. Instead, the toxins were produced as simple breakdown products of normal metabolism. They got excreted and just happened to inhibit the growth of other fungi.

She handed Jeff a number of photomicrographs, which he and Carmen looked at closely. "Where are you now on this?" he asked.

"I should have some pure crystals in a couple of days for structural analysis, then we can run toxicity tests with it."

"I like exciting new, Emily, thanks.," Jeff said to an open door. Emily had already disappeared.

Jeff didn't know who to call first, Henry, or the Chatfields. They must be wondering if he had survived the death threats. Accounting for the time difference, he thought about texting both parties, but he had too much to say and texting was a coldly impersonal way to enter back into their lives. He solved the problem when he called Henry but received no answer and no chance to leave a message. So he called Steven and Grace and turned on the video. Carmen sat by his side. Steven picked up.

"Jeffrey, how nice to hear from you," he announced. Jeff saw Grace leaning over Steven's shoulder.

Jeff introduced Carmen, who waved and Steven said, "Jeffrey, how in the world did you land such a beauty?"

This was a normal response when one compared Carmen's flawless skin and dark beauty to Jeff's shaved head, high cheekbones, Asian-like eyes, and the scar in his forehead. The scar ran above the left eye where a stalactite had gouged him while caving.

"I could ask you the same thing, Steven," Jeff offered. Everyone laughed.

Jeff explained the latest developments to Steven, or more correctly, all that had not developed. He told of his search through the records, the third threat, and their suspicion of Abbot. He concluded on an upbeat note by explaining their progress on the strange orange mold sample in Emily's possession.

Steven remained silent, thinking it over, and said, "Jeffrey, old boy, listen. Why don't you tell me more about this Abbot character and exactly where he is staying and I'll see what I can find out for you. And let me know if you get any more calls, exact date and time."

Jeff agreed to the request and the conversation changed to more comfortable talk about international relations and parties with the fishermen. The lengthy chat finally ended with Steven's promise to relay Jeff's story to Henry.

Three weeks later Jeff received another threat.

There was no change to the recorded message. He found it texted on his cell and on his message phone at the office. Both occurred at approximately 11:00 pm. Jeff texted the information to Steven who called him six days later. "Jeff, Abbot is not your man. Sorry."

Amazed that Steven had such connections to make such a claim, Jeff could only say, "How do you know for certain?"

Steven chuckled and began his tale. "A number of years ago, I accidentally ran into a toughened retired police detective who'd worked the south side of Los Angeles for most of his career and was looking for another job. He turned out to be just the man I needed for my company to handle certain internal matters, so I hired him at a good salary. After he retired, we stayed in touch.

"I called him about your problem and we arranged for him to get thrown into the half-way house and even share a room with Abbot. The two bonded like superglue and traded war stories about their detective days. My man says Abbot never used the phone a single time and didn't want revenge against anybody, but he did fear for his life as soon as he left the half-way house, because he owed a lot of money. Apparently, when he served with the police department, he sold small arms to minority groups in Oklahoma City and Tulsa, many of which were used to shoot and even kill police. The man was unpopular all the way around.

"At the time you said your call came in, the men

were in bed telling stories. The day after I told my man about your call, he said Abbot didn't make it. The following day he walked out the front door, entered a waiting car, and drove away, never to be seen again. Right now he's probably back at home watching the telly. He did ask me to thank you for the little adventure. And no, Abbot did not have an accent, unless you want to call Alabama a foreign country."

Jeff gave up on trying to figure out who initiated the threats and decided to join Emily in the lab researching the new orange fungus that refused to produce spores, yet somehow managed get from one place to another. Did it fragment under dry conditions to be carried on the wind? Preliminary experiments suggested the new mold possessed extremely high toxicity. Perhaps he could run some simple experiments to get more information.

"I stayed up late last night and searched the literature online. I can tell you it hasn't been descrbed," Emily said, as Jeff walked in wearing his lab coat.

Jeff took a flask of tiny brine shrimp commonly used to test toxicities and prepared a sample with a known number of shrimp in it. Holding his breath, he weighed a couple of the almost weightless orange crystals and added them to the solution. A quarter hour later he tried to count the number of shrimp again to find none were alive.

"That's crazy," he mumbled.

"What, doctor?" Emily asked, coming over to see

what he was talking about.

Jeff shook his head in disbelief. "It's far more toxic than aflatoxin B1, the most potent mycotoxin known and we've just started playing with this. You do it." he requested.

Emily repeated the experiment and came up with same results.

This time they tried it again using their stock of aflatoxin B1 and confirmed his suspicions.

The team set up several flasks to grow a large quantity of the strange life form in order to extract more crystalline toxin. In a week, they had enough to conduct a series of grand experiments, which they had planned for during the waiting period. Enthusiastically, Jeff shared his findings with his friends in India. Steven became particularly animated. The industry constantly sought new life forms from which new medications could be gleaned to treat an endless list of medical problems. Most new life forms had yet to be discovered in the forests and jungles of the world, although it had been known for millennia that many toxic agents in low doses have curative effects.

The next step would be to find out how this toxin worked. Did it destroy the cell membrane or bind to DNA? Steven couldn't wait for Jeff's latest reports, but knew better than to suggest Jeff turn over the project to his people. He did offer to have one of his most experienced scientists come down to assist in the investigation, to which Jeff acceded.

Jeff did not have an ego problem, per se. He did,

however, have a problem with giving a newborn child to someone else to care for and raise. A nanny in the house would be allowed.

Several days later, a suited simple-appearing pale skin gray-haired man of average height in his mid-to-late fifties appeared at the door of the institute. He introduced himself as Arnold Kaufman, displaying credentials and a letter from the senior vice president of Chatfield pharmaceuticals. Kaufman had a slight German accent.

Jeff interviewed Kaufman, to whom he immediately took a liking. The man had an honest smile and offered a wealth of ideas on how to move most efficiently on the project. "As you can imagine, it frequently takes years to develop a good pharmaceutical, even one with promise. Other times, political circumstances and public emergencies force us to do it almost overnight," Kaufman offered, smiling slightly.

Kaufman downturned his mouth in surprise at the amount of information Jeff told him about the life form and its toxicity and asked to see the lab where Jeff conducted the research. Jeff gave his guest a tour of his facility and a walk-through of the lab earmarked for the study of their new orange friend.

In the following weeks, Kaufman worked with Emily creating elegant experimental designs to allow them to study six variables simultaneously. This freed Jeff to tend to necessary, but loathsome administrative duties.

At one point in their work, Kaufman asked Emily,

"So, I understand you play music?"

"Yes, I dabble a little," she replied, surprised a stranger knew about her private life. Carmen probably told him.

"Ah, like I dabble in science," said, Kaufman, grinning. "Who do you enjoy playing most?"

"Mozart and Bach, of course, although I am particularly intrigued by Paginini," she responded, rapidly becoming pleased to find someone who had an interest in music as a working partner.

Kaufman's hand went to his mouth in a gentle touch of surprise, in quite the European gesture. "We must speak more of this some time. I once knew someone with similar tastes."

"They don't anymore?" Emily queried.

"No, she died in a car accident some 30 years ago," he responded, wistfully. Recovering quickly, he abruptly added, "Sorry to be so morose. Let us get back to work, shall we?"

One month after their conversation, Emily announced that, even though she always found time to practice, she still needed to take three days off to prepare for a concert in OKC. Kaufman inquired about the event and asked if he could attend.

"I know you can afford it and I feel a little embarrassed by doing this, but when I get a chance, I'll get you a ticket," she informed him, to his great delight. When she did, it turned out to be front row center in the packed 800 seat auditorium. The final piece played in the concert featured one of the most difficult violin concertos written, double-stringed with plucking, Paginini's *God Save the King,* featuring Emily Harrison. She stood to take a bow to a standing ovation, Kaufman among the first to rise.

Duly impressed and delighted beyond words, Kaufman went backstage to congratulate Emily who accepted his invitation for desert at an all-night diner back in Norman. Tomorrow would be Sunday and with nothing pressing in the lab the following day, they spoke of the different composers who wrote violin concertos until Emily left for home and Kaufman drove to his nearby hotel.

Jeff left the day-to-day operations to Carmen and returned to the lab to speed their rate of discovery. All partners moved smoothly and efficiently, keeping intimate records of their successes and failures. Within short months, the team received information about the unusual chemical structure of the toxin from an independent agency. Jeff had begun writing a number of scientific papers about the mold, which, by nomenclature standards would bear his name as the discoverer. To make certain of this, he had assigned one of his researchers to find if such a mold had been discovered before. Certainly, there many life forms grew on petroleum-derived products, including glue-down mastic beneath water-damaged flooring tiles, but none proliferated on tar paper outdoors with a bright orange color.

The next steps would be the most difficult: To see exactly how the toxin acted on living cells. The three scientists published several papers in peer-reviewed journals. Immediately upon their release and for the next several weeks, the institute began to receive calls and emails from other scientists who also noted the same orange-colored mold growing on a variety of structural materials, but had not investigated this proposed *Jeffrus shenerii* to the extent they had. Not all were pleased at the name given to the life form, insisting it was merely a simple mutant of another species, of which one they couldn't be sure, but they'd find out. Being protective and possessive creatures, scientists are reluctant to give credit to another. However, the thoroughness of the research spoke for itself.

Jeff pondered the larger problem with Carmen, his resident medical doctor, sweetheart, and business partner. The couple sat on their home porch on a fine Oklahoma evening. Jeff's two dogs lay by their side as they looked out at their fenced-in yard with forest on three sides and Lake Thunderbird only a few miles to the east.

"New life forms show up on occasion, even globally," Carmen offered. "Look how fast the COVID-19 pandemic spread. And don't tell me this is any different because it's a mold."

"I'm totally fine with what you're saying. But diseases like COVID tend to have a point source of origin. It spread so fast, in part, because it traveled inside people's lungs who flew everywhere, so we helped spread it outward from somewhere. This could be our case, except I can't fathom a point source for this."

"Unless there are several," Carmen contributed.

This gave Jeff pause to think. "Good point. I've had some 47 inquiries since our publication." He pulled out a piece of paper from his pocket and unfolded it. He read, "Some 75% are from the farther northern and southern polar regions such as Alaska, Russia and Siberia, Greenland, Australia, and even South Africa and southern Argentina. Is it luck of the draw or do the locations mean anything?"

"Not enough data points to make a conclusion," Carmen opined.

Jeff scratched his head. "On the other hand, maybe it's a clue. What's different about those areas from the rest of the planet?" Answering his own question, he said, "Some are lot colder than others, and some, like South Africa have every climate extreme. Nope, I'm stuck in a rut."

"Honey, why is it so important to you. It's not like this thing is causing diseases," Carmen offered.

"None we know of. That's what bothers me," Jeff replied, with a note of concern.

"Don't be so droll," she said, "Maybe it started growing on oil slicks in the ocean and the wind is spreading it."

"Where would it come from to start with?" Jeff inquired.

"I don't know. Maybe it came from a volcanic explosion," she suggested.

"That's not a bad idea," Jeff admitted. "I could tell you a lot about volcanic explosions."

"I'll bet you could," Carmen agreed, all too

readily. The man had an endless number of stored factoids.

"Did you know that virtually all major climate changes on Earth over the past hundreds of years to hundreds of millions of years can be traced to those eruptions? A single explosion releases more greenhouse gases into the world's atmosphere than everything man has ever emitted with his pollutants? Remind me to check on the number of oil spills in the various oceans in recent years," he concluded.

Well accustomed to Jeff's eccentric ramblings, Carmen said, softly, "I'll keep that in mind. Honey, here's another brilliant idea. How about if you focus on taking care of me?" she teased, running her fingernails lightly over the nape of his neck.

Three

Jeff gave up trying to figure out the origin of the new life form until he had more information. Meanwhile, Emily and Kaufman were a regular feature in the lunchroom and weekly deliveries of cosmetics and personal care products still came in from around the country for analysis. These samples consisted of toothpaste, eye shadow, skin toner, face cream, sun screen, aftershave, blush, deodorant, foot powder, shampoo, conditioner, and literally any skin-care product. These were representative of batches slated for public usage, which meant nobody in the country could use a damn thing until Jeff said it was safe to do so.

When he accepted the task assigned to him

by a representative of the Consumer Product Safety Commission, he didn't think that kind of responsibility would be his alone. Yet, someone had named him Mr. Clearinghouse, a title he loathed. He wasn't afraid of responsibility, per se, and didn't shy away from the millions the government sunk into the program. He did want to spend more time in pure research, not in business management.

Once the samples were found to be clear of mycotoxins, they were discarded in a designated dumpster. Meticulous records were maintained in duplicate, which required an add-on room for their storage and the hiring of a records manager.

Of the hundreds of samples thus far analyzed none had been found to contain mycotoxin, until one did.

Two of his lab-coated scientists approached Jeff in his office with the news. One of them, Jim, held a tube of toothpaste, and another man, David, held a number of machine printouts. Jim said, "It's positive for Roridin A, doctor. We triple checked."

Jeff swiveled his chair from his desk to face Jim and held out his hand to receive the tube. Turning it back to front he saw it had standard labeling: large brand name on a blue oval background with the added words: SPECIAL INGREDIENTS FOR TEETH WHITENING. In small print on the reverse were words: Active Ingredients: baking soda, peroxide. The inactive ingredients included the usual preservatives and anti-microbial agents. Below it all in small print were the three words: Made in Mexico.

Jeff handed back the tube and took the printouts from Dave depicting a graph with a large spike. On the papers someone had written his name, date, time, batch number, and the words Roridin A. Jeff knew Roridin A was produced by the mold *Fusarium*, a contaminant of grains such as wheat, oats, and maize. It had no business being in toothpaste unless somebody put it there. The toxin was in the same class as the one produced by numerous mold species including *Stachybotrys,* the much maligned black mold. The fact that it came from another country opened up a can of worms, not for Jeff, but for the nation. It meant other products made by the same company had to be screened, as did other imported products. It also meant more bad guys needed to be tracked down.

Jeff said, "I'm surprised they couldn't come up with something more original. What's the concentration of the toxin?"

"It's low," answered Dave.

Jeff nodded slowly in understanding. "Slow burn, won't be immediately yanked from the shelves or discovered for some time."

What a mess. Jeff returned to the lab with the two men who took him through the standardized series of tests they conducted numerous times daily. At least this time he didn't have to personally get involved, wind up in jail, get into fist fights, have a shotgun pointed at him, or have his dogs chew up somebody trying to burn down his house. But as he likes to say when things are going too smoothly, "The day is still young."

"When did this come in?" asked Jeff.

"Sometime over the weekend, I guess," Jim replied.

"I thought we got our shipments on Wednesday," Jeff said.

"The boxes were stacked beneath the rear portico, as usual," Dave answered.

"Where are the other boxes?" Jeff asked.

"Everybody's working on them," answered Jim.

Another worker appeared at the doorway and announced, "Doctor, I was looking for you. We've got a positive for Roridin A in this eye shadow."

Jeff's hackles rose. He quickly picked up the phone and told Carmen to sound the signals for an emergency meeting. He wanted all staff members in the conference room. This meant everyone had five minutes to quit what they were doing.

Jeff went directly to the designated room and took a seat at the head of the table as a full dozen lab-coated staff members took their seats. Aside from old Arnie, their gofer, Carmen was the only one without the lab coat, notepad in hand, her long black tresses trailing behind her Indian print blouse, turquoise skirt and blue sneakers like a flower at the end of an oval of white surrounding an oval of brown.

Jeff addressed Arnie first. "Arnie, how many cases did you find this morning?"

"Twelve, sir," he answered. "I dropped two off outside each of the labs and slit them open."

"Jim, Dave, you reported first. How many tubes were in your box," Jeff inquired.

"Twenty four," Jim answered.

Others reported in turn, "We got the eye shadow."

"We got the blush."

"We got the aftershave."

Jeff held up his hand. Eight more cases of different personal care products awaited analysis. Obviously, these would take precedence over the standard fare they had been receiving. Did this chance discovery justify all their efforts—again, less talented persons could have come up with the same results.

"Somebody's playing games with us," Jeff said. "I suspect the entire new batch is contaminated. Only touch the one's you're working with and report to me your findings in detail—printouts, everything. Then sample two others from your batch. Three total. Don't touch any of the others. By the end of the day, we're probably going to need the feds."

Jeff concluded, "They'll need fingerprint samples from the untested jars and tubes, so, other than the three you use, keep your hands off of them. Now, let's get back to work."

Jeff reviewed the video feed of the drop-off. He saw a man in a hoodie driving a white panel van with no license plate take out boxes from the back at 2:45 a.m. Nothing solid there, but he'd pass it on.

Jeff returned to his office and tried to think it though. It appeared as though the threat were tied to the shipment. After all, the male voice said he was going to destroy Jeff, not kill him. Where was the point of sending him all the bad stuff? Were they sending him a messsage saying they could do what they wanted when they wanted? Everything in the marketplace had to go through Jeff's institute anyway before it got approved. Granted there was a backlog … unless distribution might be occurring without Jeff's approval. Might they be seeing more name brands with poison in them. Or, perhaps manufacturers were buying generic ingredients, which unbeknownst to them, were laced with poison to bypass Jeff's inspection in order to avoid a lag in sales.

He decided against trying to figure out all the intricacies of the scheme. One thing he did feel certain about. Somebody was putting a lot of money into this venture and he had a target on his back with national shame as a reward for his efforts. Once the poisons took hold, millions of people could be affected and Mr. Clearinghouse would be blamed.

After turning over the bad samples to the authorities, lab work returned to the screening of regular shipments and Jeff returned to the business of working with Emily and Kaufman on the orange fungus.

They soon found by diluting the concentration of the crystals 1000-fold over what he had used the growth rate of bacteria was slowed without killing them. They found the rate of reproduction of rapidly growing bacteria was slowed more than that of slower growing bacteria. In fact, the faster the cells reproduced, the slower the rate of reproduction.

Kaufman said they already had drugs like that against tumors, but those tended to cause side effects in humans and weren't nearly as effective as the one in their possession. He also surmised it might be used where other cells proliferated abnormally, such as in leukemia.

But, as in all experiments of this kind, what happens in a test tube doesn't always translate into what happens in biological systems. What dosage of a medication can be used without harming the patient? If harm is to be expected, what is the nature of that harm?

Meanwhile, more reports about the new fungus were received from polar regions than from equatorial regions. A concentration of anything is highest nearest the source, whether it be a point source of radioactivity, following the size of gold nuggets in a stream to find the mother lode, or a strange orange mold that appears out of nowhere.

To Kaufman, it didn't matter where it came from. It is what it is. He wanted to turn the project over to his people who could put a score of scientists to work on it immediately. Jeff wasn't ready for that. After discussing the matter with the Emily and Kaufman one day, he brought up the subject of its origin once again.

Emily offered, "We have to tie in what is happening in the polar regions today that hasn't happened before, right? We already know our orange friend loves petroleum and long-chain hydrocarbons. I say it might be tied to oil spills in the ocean in some way."

Jeff said, "Carmen thought the same thing."

"Maybe a combination of oil and colder water helps it reproduce," Kaufman offered.

"We already tried growing it in the lab under various temperatures with and without oil, and its growth slows at lower temperatures," Jeff said. He began to pace and added, "We're thinking inside the box. Maybe it lived someplace all along and something changed to expose it to the air, like removing centuries of dirt to find a buried city."

The three almost said the word at the same instant, as realization struck them. *Permafrost.* Jeff began to expound, "The warming of the polar regions is exposing trillions of tons of early vegetation and organic material. Ages of frozen ice are melting."

"And seeping up from beneath the permafrost is layers of oil with pockets of methane gas created by bacteria that are digesting the organic material," Emily threw in, excitedly, reaching up to push her eyeglasses back in place. "Want to see global warming? Just wait until all the methane hits the atmosphere."

Kaufman got into it the conversationt and said, "Which means we may have untold riches awaiting us in terms of new life forms emend cures for diseases."

Jeff philosophized, "Everything that makes sense isn't always true. It's an interesting theory we might want to present. We need more data, then I'll consider letting you, Arnold, have *Jeffrus shererii* to take back to your company. Meanwhile, I'm going to talk to some friends in India."

When he did, he called Henry first, who said Raj wanted him to come for another dinner and take a ride into the jungle with him to look for new species to discover. And the village chief would throw another party in honor of their Hollywood friend. At the mention of both offers, Jeff's stomach began to rumble.

Four

Standing at the kitchen counter, facing Carmen, Jeff said, "Honey, don't look a gift horse in the mouth. Take things at face value."

"What does that mean?" Carmen retorted, inhaling, eyebrows raised, nostrils flaring.

"When somebody gives you something, don't examine it too closely because you might be disappointed." Jeff pointed to a small box wrapped securely in expensive paper from a well-known seller of high-end women's personal care products based in Philadelphia. Carmen's name and address were clearly printed.

"It just came. I haven't even opened it yet and you're after me," she retorted. "Jeff, I know this company."

Jeff took a step back and pushed his palms downward. "Look, honey, with everything going on with the threats and the toxins delivered to us, and the FBI involved, and the whole thing blowing up, we need to think about your safety."

"Jeff, don't be stupid. You're not here when

this comes. It's an auto-ship that arrives every two months. It's just cleansing cream and eye shadow."

"And it's been two months since your last shipment?" he inquired.

"About, I guess, why?"

"Can you do me a favor and check, please?"

"No, I'm not going to check," Carmen said, emphatically. "You're being paranoid and it's starting to bother me."

Jeff picked up the package, then said, "Sorry, baby, I'll make it up to you." He departed, listening to his sweetheart come out with such a stream of invective in Spanish that he lost track of what she was saying after the first three words, none of which were polite.

Great, just great, Jeff thought as he went through the gears on his supercharged Mustang on the way out to the lake. He needed to get away. He had to take off his shoes, sit on the shore, watch the ducks, and think. He wanted to analyze the contents of the box on his own, but he was afraid Carmen would say he rigged the results to make things go his way. So he had turned over the box to a local OKC independent laboratory for analysis on a rush order. Hell, he didn't even know what could be in the box to start with. It would never have passed through the U.S. mail if it were a pressurized canister or explosives. Maybe he overreacted, but damn, he loved Carmen so much he would rather put up with her wrath than to see harm befall her.

After four days of putting op with her anger, and

on the verge of calling the analytical company, he finally received an email that read:

Dr. Shenero: We apologize for the delay in processing your rush order, but our initial analysis required further confirmation from a second larboratory. Within the box we found three quality products for women, all of which contained Roridin A, the mycotoxin you asked us to look for. It's in an extremely high concentration. I'm sure you are aware that if used, these products will result in permanent scarring and pitting of the face along with blindness. Please find the attachments for the reports for each of the three products from each of two laboratories. We will retain the samples and the cover wrap for your pickup, as per your request. I am available to discuss this project at your convenience.

FYI, we also found an embossed card with a generic statement that read: We hope our products meet your expectations.

Signed,
Chris Matthews
Chief Technician
Biochemical Analytics

Jeff downloaded the reports and printed everything, then he drove up to the city to pick up the box of samples and the original reports. He followed that by driving to the local FBI office to give them a copy of all written documents pertaining to the case, along with a copy of the video of the van dropping off the parcels, before returning to work.

During the drive he tried to formulate a plan. In a few minutes he would have to tell Carmen the bad news. Somebody knew where she lived. They were trying to cause great angst for him with her serving as the moving target.

When he arrived home, he saw Carmen's Toyota in the drive. He found her in the kitchen preparing dinner, her back to him. Another package stood on the counter identical to the first. "Hi, what's this?" he said simply.

"They made a mistake and sent me another shipment," she replied, without turning around. "You can take that one too, if you want."

Enough is enough. Jeff threw down the copy of the email and lab printouts on the counter. "Read these." It was not a request.

Sighing, Carmen turned around and picked up the papers without looking at him and went from one to the other until her shoulders slumped. She finally looked at him with sadness in her eyes. She threw down the papers and wrapped her arms around him. "I'm so sorry I didn't believe you," she cried, with honest tears borne of guilt flowing freely, Pulling away, she said, "But what's this other one, I mean ...."

"Most likely, it's your regular shipment. If it's all right with you, I'll have this one tested, as well. Where do you order these from, office or home?" he asked.

"Well, I haven't placed an order for a long time because it's all auto-shipped," she replied. "You're not here when they come."

Jeff nodded, "Which suggests our computer has been hacked." He added, "Come on, it's over. Forget dinner. I'm ready for some Mississippi gumbo?"

Jeff did not consider himself to be a well-balanced person. Neither did anyone else. He was obsessive about his work, protective, vindictive, vengeful, and relentless. If at all possible, he personally would figure out the persons behind this and hurt them. One line of reasoning said there may not be mass poisonings after all. First, the deliveries were made so he could find the poison. It might be in the marketplace, but no recalls had been reported. He saw it as an expensive and sick prank with no consequences to the public at large.

The products sent to Carmen at home were of the same vein, except the perpetrators believed she would use them, in fact, they wanted her to use them. That pissed him off.

The guy on the recording with the slight accent was likely from the Middle East. He'd heard enough of their languages to hazard a fair guess, either that or he had spent a lot of early years there. He was definitely not a good ole' boy from Arkansas or the Louisiana Bayou. Therefore, if the Middle East were his place of origin and he wanted to play the mycotoxin game, he must have been affiliated with the MaHood's who engineered the poisoned newspaper ink fiasco—perhaps a stray man who slipped through the cracks of Interpol, CIA, FBI, Homeland Security, and bounty hunters.

What to do? There were too many moving parts for one person to be involved. If his home computer were hacked, then an expert might be able to find a clue as to who did it. It that were the case, the bad guys must have thought they hit the jackpot when they discovered Carmen's standing order for the cosmetics. So they purchased their own items, added the poisons, and shipped them earlier than she would expect in the same box they came in. When she got the regular shipment a week or ten days later, she would either keep it or return it. In any case, there was a strong likelihood Carmen would lose a good part of her face sooner or later once she began to use the new products.

Thinking it through, he reasoned that if his computer were hacked, he didn't notice any of the telltale signs, such as sudden slowing, pop-ups, programs not connecting properly, sluggish cursor, and another half-dozen indicators. But what did he know? He needed a game plan. He would take it to a friend of his at the university who taught computer science. Then he'd know for certain. And then what? Set a trap? Surely the bad guy must be watching closely to see the fruits of his labor.

Three days later, Jeff called Steven Chatfield in India and discussed the situation with him, because Steven had earlier declared he wanted to be all in. In fact, his avocation was helping people through difficult times. What's the point of having money and connections if you can't do good with them?

Steven told Jeff to give him a few days to set it up, which Jeff did. Then the pair launched the plan.

As per plan, Jeff emailed Steven from the home computer, the same one Carmen used to place orders.

Dear Steven: As I told you on the phone, we haven't received any more bad products, but I'm afraid my reputation will be ruined if this keeps up. To make matters worse, since I last spoke with you, Carmen has somehow gotten a terrible rash on her face and her eyes burn. She refuses to leave the house and I can't blame her. The rash gets worse daily. The doctors I speak with ask endless questions, but don't give answers. Do you have any suggestions? I'm desperate.

Dear Jeff: As a matter of fact, I can recommend a terrific product. It's so new it's not yet in the pharmacies, but you can order it online. It's called Face Clear by C.K. Pharmaceuticals (www. ckpharmaceuticals.com). It's an excellent anti-inflammatory and it's selling out fast, mainly by word of mouth, so I suggest you get right on it. Expect a delay in fulfilling your order because of their backlog, so maybe you can put a rush on it.

Regards, Steven

While Jeff set the trap, Carmen enjoyed her days off, staying out of sight, working out in the exercise room, catching up on reading, and waiting. Only two people contacted the fake corporation to order the fake product: Jeff and one other person.

Monitoring the situation, the FBI quickly tracked the owner of the email and arrested three men on terrorism charges, all Saudi nationals.

Dear Steven: I must say you have exceeded yourself. If you read the papers, you'd have seen the little manufacturing plant these guys had in their basement. From what I'm told, they believed I would be looking for Aflatoxin like the first time, so they hired a microbiologist/chemist who went with another mycotoxin like Roridin A to throw us off. Their facility wasn't close to being big enough to go national, but served their purposes of making me chase my tail for a while. The millions they had in the bank got confiscated and another half-dozen of their associates were arrested here and in Saudi Arabia. Doubtless, there's more like them out there.

As you probably know, Emily and Kaufman communicate almost daily. He's offered her a job when she graduates in a couple of months and she's accepted. We'll miss her, dearly.

The next time I find some old mold on your property, I'll name it after you. Thank you so much for your kind assistance.

Say hello to Grace and Henry.

Warmest, Jeff

Dear Jeff: You've already returned the favor in spades. We believe the orange life form you gave us has great potential to cure or assist in the curing of many diseases. In addition, my people tell me it may have action on the telomeres. This would be huge. In fact, it's just what we've been looking for and we've shifted another six of our scientists over to 'Orange Department' as we named it, with Kaufman at the helm. (From what I hear, he is anxiously awaiting Emily's arrival!)

Drop by next time you're in the neighborhood and passing through Bimli.

Regards from Grace and Henry.

Steven

When Jeff read the email, he thought, *Whoa! Telomeres are DNA-protein complexes at the end of each chromosome and the amino acid phenylalanine is a big part of the complex. Telomeres shorten upon aging, which means that in the tiniest trace amounts of my Agent Orange, it might slow the aging process.*

What was it he used to tell his students? *Welcome to the world of the fungi and the molds. They can poison you to death. They can make you sneeze or bring down a building. They can cure whatever ails you or get you burned at the stake. They make bread and alcohol and at the same time, destroy billions of dollars of crops each year. Do not underestimate them.*

Shipboard

One

The day was fairly average for this time of the year in San Diego, in the low 70s, ocean breeze south-south west at 7 mph. Jeff and Carmen stood on the bank holding hands looking at the monster in front of them bragging nine decks above the water line with another three below it, 240,000 gross tons of weight, 24 million cubic feet of cruise ship and 320 cooks. They only needed to meet up with one of them, the Executive Chef, as his designated guests for the voyage.

At 10:00 am, and escorted by a ship's mate, the couple stood at the head of one of the lines of some 6000 guests on one of two gangways. Once past security, the mate led them to an elevator that would take them to the very top their larger first class cabin at the front of the ship considered prime real estate. From there they could have an excellent view of the ocean and any upcoming ports of call. This was opposed to the least expensive interior cubicles enclosed by four walls with no views. These comprised the highest percentage of accommodations.

Each cabin had about the same interior size, but exterior suites had a balcony with chairs and railing. Almost all, however, had the same amenities including TV, vanity, shower, commode, blow-dryer, pull-out desk, and two beds, in most cases. In the unit assignd to Jeff and Carmen, a sofa occupied one wall. On one of the beds, two swans made of towels faced each other with their heads touching. Supposedly, a dozen figures could be created.

At that moment, a pleasant young woman introduced herself as the cabin steward for the floor. She would be straightening up at least once daily unless they hung a "Do Not Disturb" sign on the door. She would be pleased to provide them whatever they required. Carmen requested a bottle of Chardonnay on ice and the smiling woman departed.

The couple unpacked the few belonging needed for the voyage, and, armed with maps and guides, left their suite to explore the floating city—complete in all regards, they would soon discover.

Pierre LaMonde served as the Executive Chef onboard. A year earlier, his wife had called Jeff from Oklahoma City, where their relatives also lived. A pipe had broken in a bathroom and although a plumber had stopped the flow, a remediation company told her it would be some time before they got to the home because the passage of a recent bad storm was keeping all remediation companies busy. By the time anyone did arrive, the room smelled musty. The wife called Jeff to conduct his tests and to advise the company on how he wanted procedures to be conducted; no ifs, ands, or buts.

While at the house, the wife was preparing guacamole in the kitchen with their eight-year-old daughter, who put the pit in her mouth to suck off the remaining avocado. The mother didn't see it and asked her a question. When the daughter tried to speak, she swallowed the pit and it lodged in her throat. The mother tried slapping her on the back, but the pit remained stuck. Jeff heard the commotion and grabbed the girl from behind beneath her arms with his fists in the sternum area and yanked upward a couple of times to dislodge the pit.

Several days later Jeff received a call from LaMonde insisting that he and another person of his choice be his guest on a cruise, all expenses paid. After months of badgering from Carmen, Jeff relented and informed LaMonde they would be happy to take him up on his offer.

They had both been to San Diego before and had noticed the cruise ships, having chatted about one day going aboard one, but never imagined they would be wined and dined by the what was arguably—excluding the captain and the engineering staff—the second-most important person on the vessel serving under the hotel manager.

The Cruise line had assigned LaMonde to work this trip at this time, as opposed to the Caribbean tour or even the world tour, although any cruise Jeff and Carmen chose would be fine with him. If they chose this one, he would personally meet them the following morning once things settled down. Now the time belonged to them for exploration.

On the balcony outside their room, Carmen stood at the glass-enclosed patio with the railing some four feet in height. Carmen opened out the schematic of the vessel to review. Reading the legend, she said, excitedly, "Where do we start, honey? Let's see, 35 restaurants, food 24-hours a day, theaters, magic shows, casinos, auctions, libraries, gyms, a full-size basketball court, a rock-climbing wall, 15 swimming pools, 30 places to eat, a 1000 seat auditorium, salons, jewelry stores . . . it's an entire floating city. It even has a helipad and a park. In addition to the guests, there's a crew of 2315. I mean, how can anybody not like this?"

Jeff laughed at Carmen's enthusiasm. "You sound like a salesperson for the cruise line. I know several people who didn't enjoy their trip. Their rooms were small and cramped, the hallways narrow, the noise of all the activities was annoying, or they got seasick, and people were everywhere they went."

Carmen folded the schematic and put it in her purse. Grabbing Jeff's arm, she said, "Fine. Let them find fault. We're going to have a good time. I'm ready to play tourist."

Three hours later the ship left port and began the

travel north toward Ketchikan, Alaska, traveling at a speed of approximately 25 mph. First stop, Seattle, over two days away. Plans called for them to disembark mid-morning of the third day for sightseeing, and to return by evening to continue onward. The entire journey would be unusual in that the cruise would not only take them to the usual Alaskan ports, but would return down, bypassing San Diego, with Puerto Vallarta, Mexico, on the list of stops before returning to home base. The entire journey was scheduled for a full two weeks.

The following morning at 7:30, the pair found the reserved table at a restaurant designated by LaMonde and began eating their breakfasts of fruit, yogurt and coffee, deciding to save their big appetites for later. The selections had not been easy in this one room already serving customers in an obscenely overcrowded buffet. With six servers behind the breakfast buffet bar, virtually every taste was catered to from sea foods, dairy, meat lover's paradise, starch lovers paradise, breakfast cereals, and fruit salads.

They made an interesting-appearing couple. Jeff was well-tanned from outdoor jogging. He wore loose-fitting white pants and sneakers with a blue polo shirt, while Carmen wore similar garb with one of her Indian print blouses. Indeed, they had drawn eyes the afternoon and evening before when Jeff's face and Carmen's beauty stood out. Many recognized him because his picture had been in many newspapers and television broadcasts.

Not long before, Jeff had unmasked a great terrorist plot and the government had confiscated billions in assets. At the time, Carmen had received several requests for interviews and to appear on the cover of various fashion magazines. She declined the offers. She did not like to show off her beauty, which didn't stop the publication of their photos captured by photographers hidden behind trees.

Pierre LaMonde stood about five inches shorter than Jeff's 5'-11". He wore all white with no hat, as was the custom of the head chef. According to his wife, she had met him shortly after she had won the Miss Lebanon contest. At that time, the French-born Pierre grew up in Lebanon and aspired to greatness as a cook, so they move to France where he went to culinary school. He became a 5-Star-rated head chef and after a dozen years, ran across an ad from the cruise lines. They needed executive chefs.

LaMonde sent in his resume and got hired immediately. That was years ago. He spoke English, French, Arabic, and Spanish, and had stories galore. That is, if one were patient enough to put up with the garrulous man. Reportedly, he could regale one with the latest cruise-ship happenings and hear-say, including ribald stories about crew members.

When he appeared, Jeff stood to shake his hand. LaMonde, perhaps in his mid-fifties, shifted his eyes to Carmen, who remained seated, apprised her instantly, and asked Spanish if she spoke Spanish. When she replied in Spanish, LaMonde took a seat at the table and the two conversed for several minutes with Jeff enjoying the exchange. People can instantly like or be put off by the other.

Jeff and Carmen frequently spoke Spanish at home and he followed the exchange when LaMonde asked her, "Do you know the difference between a shark and cruise ship passenger?"

Puzzled at the question, she smiled slightly, shaking her head no. Jeff had heard the joke, and waited in amusement for the punch line.

LaMonde said, "One constantly searches various waters for food, never satisfied, surveys the food for some time, or attacks instantly to eat beyond fullness. The other is a fish."

Jeff grinned as Carmen burst out in laughter.

Returning to English, Carmen said, "You must have a lot of stories."

"Oh, one or two more, perhaps," laughed LaMonde. "Here's another one. This goes back a few years before things changed a little. A retired woman lived on a fixed income. She was bored living alone and her grown children didn't want her to move in with them. In fact, they suggested she move into an assisted living home. Instead, she decided to take a cruise. She like it so much she sold her home and signed up for a lifetime onboard ship, traveled the world, ate like a horse, met new people all the time and saved money on gas, car and home insurance, and so forth.

"She had free time because she didn't have to drive anywhere. Plus, if you're living onboard, there's no place to keep what you buy anyway, except for a new dress once in a while or a small picture. Wherever she stopped, she made a habit of sending her children a post card saying, 'having a great time, wish you were here.' We're talking about Amsterdam, Singapore, Hong Kong, Chile, Calcutta, Bangkok, South Africa, you name it. They were green with envy."

Jeff didn't like the glint in Carmen's eye and quickly changed the subject. "Depending on your time, could you point out the highlights for us and what to look for on the cruise? he asked."

Jeff saw LaMonde as a treasure trove of information and wanted to probe the depths of the man's knowledge while he had the chance. He asked, "Pierre, this beautiful ship can't last forever. What will happen to it someday?"

La Monde grinned. "Ah, yes, there is that. Hundreds of ships die each year, many are smaller older freighters, others are cruise ships of different sizes that can be retrofitted and turned into hotels. But most end up on the shores of India or Pakistan or Bangladesh for salvage or to rot away offshore. It is a sad ending."

"India, huh? I know a little about that country. What coast, east or west," Jeff became intrigued.

"Just up the coast from Mumbai is the world's largest ship graveyard," La Monde answered. "It's dangerous work."

For some unexplained reason, Jeff found a fascination with the subject. He'd never thought about it until this point in time and now he couldn't learn enough. He wanted to ask more of the chef but thought better of it. Maybe another time.

LaMonde started to say something else, but caught himself.

Jeff knew the charismatic chef would treat them to a memorable vacation. How memorable, he had no idea. Once again, La Monde began to speak, then caught himself a second time.

Jeff said, "All right, Pierre, out with it. What's on your mind?"

"I'm a little embarrassed to ask this, but I need your help with something," LaMonde said, sheepishly.

Jeff quickly glanced at Carmen, who raised her eyebrows in a "Here we go," gesture.

"Come on, we're all friends here," Jeff replied. He immediately regretted the use of that sentence. It reminded him of time share salespersons whose sole purpose was to con people into upgrading what they already owned, never to be sold by them again.

"Yes, please, Pierre. Tell us. We'll do what we can to help," Carmen added. She liked this man as a person. He gave off good honest vibes, something not often run across in today's world, as least in her view.

"It's a problem," said LaMonde.

"We all have problems," Jeff returned.

"It's a medical problem," LaMonde said.

"You have a medical staff," Carmen stated.

"It's not about me. Yes, we have two doctors and

three nurses, but there are some things the cruise ship companies would rather keep quiet," LaMonde continued.

"Welcome to the real world. Pierre, do we play word games or will you please get to the point," Jeff said, glancing around to ensure no others in the crowded restaurant were within listening distance.

"Are you familiar with norovirus?" LaMonde asked.

"Of course. It's a big issue on cruise ships. Diarrhea and vomiting. Spread through food and water," Jeff answered.

"Yes. We've had it, but what's going on now is not through normal . . . ," he spoke to Carmen in Spanish and she replied, "Distribution."

"Yes, distribution," LaMonde, said. "It's not a big enough problem for the media to take the story and the company isn't reporting it, but it's costing them a fortune with quiet payoffs to settle lawsuits and some people are pointing a finger at me."

Jeff shrugged. "I'm sure there are always going to be lawsuits for a variety of reasons, what with thousands of people per ship per cruise. Besides, some claims may be valid, others not so. It's common knowledge that the norovirus hit the industry hard. I can't imagine having to scrub down an entire vessel. How many are there on the ocean these days?"

"A little over 300 of these ships, each making several trips a year serving millions of people," LaMonde said. "Not all of them were affected, but I know this particular ship got hit hard. But, again, noro is not our problem."

"Go ahead," Jeff encouraged.

LaMonde rubbed a palm over his eyes before replying, "This ship, The Princess Fairie, has five times the complaints of any of the others and almost all of the complaints are different than what the other ships are reporting."

"How do you know that?" Jeff asked,

"Come on, doctor, I've been, how do you say, around the block a few times. This ain't my first rodeo."

At that, Carmen began to laugh, followed by Jeff, and then LaMonde. The man was truly a curiosity, conversational in at least four languages who understood many others, couldn't come up with certain words, but could come up with idioms specific to a particular sect or lifestyle.

The ice had broken. LaMonde appeared to read Jeff's mind when he said "What we have is very different from norovirus. If it were noro, we'd be in deep trouble and have to report it. And you don't lie about that kind of thing."

"How do you know it's not something in the food? Sorry, had do ask," Carmen asked.

"I'm glad you did," replied LaMonde. "Because I've been in the business some 30 years and I know food problems when I see them. We have over 30 kitchens aboard ship. My duties are basically managerial. I work 12-hour days to oversee cleanliness of the kitchens that must conform to international standards. Besides, the symptoms don't match anything caused by food issues that I know of."

"Which are?" asked Carmen

"Coughing, inflamed sinus cavities, watering eyes, intermittent difficulty in breathing," answered the chef.

"Tell you what, Pierre. We've got most of the day together, so why don't you give us the tour and if we have any questions, we'll ask," Jeff offered.

"Deal," LaMonde said, pleased to change the subject. He began to stand, thought for an instant, then regained his seat. "There's more," he said, obviously embarrassed again at what he wanted to say.

"Get it out, Pierre," Jeff suggested, gently, as one friend to another.

LaMonde began, "Cruise ships deal with the same problems as everybody else in the world. Drugs. They come onboard with the initial food supplies. They could be anywhere. They get distributed among the passengers and we're at a loss as to how this thing operates."

Jeff asked, "Why kind of supplies come onboard this ship when you get ready to sail?"

LaMonde pulled out a piece of paper from his pocket and unfolded it, placing it in front of the couple. Carmen picked it up and read, "6000 gallons of soda, 20,000 pounds of chicken, 140,000 eggs, one ton coffee, 30,000 meals a day . . . "

"And that's for one week. Throw in beef, fish, fruits and vegetables, desserts, alcohol, and so forth," interrupted LaMonde. "When all that gets loaded, it gets sent to different freezers and kitchens for prep work. Think of all the sheets and pillow cases that have to be changed. That's once in a 7 day cruise and twice in a 10-14 day cruise."

"And somewhere in that mess the drugs are coming in," Carmen said. "Pierre, you have security force for that."

"True," replied the chef. "Unfortunately, I'm not sure I trust them all, but I do trust you two."

"My guess is that cocaine is the drug of choice," Jeff offered.

"Correct. That and meth and opioides. Nothing too crazy like LSD or magic mushrooms.. This is a world-wide network of dealers that supply the cruise lines with both old and new staff who move product to the on-board customers. They rake in tens of millions a week world-wide. Authorities think it's tied to food, which is me. The company needs a fall guy, but getting rid of me won't solve the problem."

"So we're looking at the movers, not the suppliers," Jeff summarized.

"Yes, that's the way I see it," LaMonde.

"If that's the case, I'll need more information from you," Jeff stated. Changing the subject, he asked, "My first question is: What's the difference between you and the head steward in terms of responsibilities?"

LaMonde answered, "There's some crossover in that we're both charged with maintaining cleanliness and sanitary conditions of the kitchens, and overseeing the staff who do so, although he is in charge of the ship's cleanliness in general. I do a lot of menu detailing and he does a lot of food ordering. All chefs report to me and I have to ensure that proper nutrition is presented in what we serve."

"By ship cleanliness, does that include the cabins, too?" asked Carmen.

"Yes. Those would be the cabin stewards," replied LaMonde. He stood to indicate the conversation had ended, apparently anxiious to give the tour, at which time Carmen slipped her arm into his, as though they were a couple.

Aside from brief breaks to check on business, LaMonde left them alone by 5:00 that evening, his obligation as a good host completed.

Two hours later, Jeff and Carmen sat dining at the captain's table along with Sven Larson, the Captain, enjoying their meal served on fine china and drinks in crystal glasses, eating lobster tail, filet mignon, prime rib, and drinking expensive wines.

They tried to digest all they had learned from LaMonde, but were unable to discuss it under the circumstances with several others present. Among them sat a European actress; another, a known writer of mystery novels; and a state senator with his wife.

At last, happy and tired after a long day, the couple retired to their cabin, each on a separate bed and lay quietly for several moments until Carmen said, "It can't be the food."

"Nope. Why anybody would blame him is beyond me," Jeff replied. "I think he's a little paranoid."

"He has a right to be. You got any ideas yet?" she asked.

"Maybe," he answered.

"I'd sure like to get my hands on the medical records," she added.

"Yep, but no can do."

"Why not?" she asked.

"Good question," Jeff said. "Maybe can do. The captain did fawn over you."

"Your reputation didn't hurt, either. Let's see what tomorrow brings," she offered.

"Sweet dreams," Jeff said, and turned off the light. In an instant he turned them on again, picked up the room phone and called the number LaMonde had given them. He spoke for a moment, listened, hung up, turned off the light, and rolled over to fall asleep.

Two

Jeff tried to reason out what LaMonde had told him about the drug problem. The issue wasn't supply or demand. Both were present in abundance. It wasn't getting the product to the customer. How it got to the customer became the issue. He doubted if anybody did the old hand-shake switcheroo between drugs vs. bills anymore because of concerns for disease transmission. To him, the basic question boiled down to this: If the customer knew coke was available, simply because it's always available just about anywhere, how does the seller let the customer know? So far, authorities had concentrated their efforts on trying to discover the source of the supply chain. Did the bad guys hide the products in hollowed out eggs, or in chicken parts, or any one of a hundred imaginative ways to hide anything? Stop the source to stop the problem. Needle in a haystack.

Jeff had closed the door behind him as they were leaving for breakfast the next morning when the room phone rang. Jeff picked it up and listened, then replaced the receiver.

"Meeting's set with the captain at 9:00. He'll have the medical records with him." he told Carmen. "We'll meet him in his suite."

Prior to the meeting, Jeff worked out in a kick boxing class that overlooked one of the surface swimming pools and the ocean beyond. As the ship cut through increasingly choppy waves, he paused in his efforts to watch the water in the pool slosh from one end to the other, shooting some 20 feet into the air before the slope of the surrounding deck drained it back into the pool, where it sloshed against the other wall. Not a good day to do laps.

Captain Sven Larson looked his name. Tall, blond, blue-eyed and Norwegian, he had been hired away from Norwegian lines at a better pay grade and had been with the new company five years. He learned from LaMonde that Carmen had a degree in medicine, albeit trained in Mexico and within a hair's breadth of getting her U.S. certification (until she met Jeff). Combining that with Jeff's reputation, coupled with the possibility of a shipboard health-related scandal, he willingly acceded to their request. His background check on the man found he had top secret security clearance with both the U.S. Goverment and Interpol. Not a bad man to share knowledge with or to learn from. One of the ship's two medical doctors stood next to the captain when Larson greeted his guests at the knock.

Earlier, Larson had opened the drapes to reveal an outer deck and the brightness of the day flooding the room, as the ship headed due north. In the distance, at the horizon, the sky appeared to darken. A squall was in progress, presently pounding Seattle with a summer storm. Passengers were advised to limit their walking and take Dramamine, if necessary, and to go to the center of the ship where the rise and fall of the vessel would be less. This is because the ship would soon be entering rougher waters. One of the seemingly endless stream of announcements advised passengers to bring along their umbrellas once they disembarked.

Before the doctor lay a stack of ten manila folders he had placed on a small table. The three took a seat while Larson stood, looking on as the doctor began to page through each of the files that contained pictures, names, addresses, medical histories, complaints, interview records and notes regarding payouts. When he had completed the first file and set it aside, Jeff said, "Excuse me, but can we do that again. I'd like to use my cell to photograph each page of each file."

The doctor looked up at the tall captain who gave the briefest of nods downward. After all, according to his extensive research on the man, this Shenero character could do whatever he wanted, as long as it didn't involve stearing the vessel.

"Yes, of course, but I can get you copies of these," the doctor offered.

"Photos will be fine," Jeff said. He had his own plan.

When the doctor finished, Carmen asked, "Did they have any common area of housing?"

"None at all," the doctor replied. "That was one of the first things we looked at. Typically, the first rooms to go are the luxury suites and the balconies. The last are the cheaper seats, the interior cabins. These people were in every area of the ship, top, bottom, middle, front, and rear. The only common thing is they all visited the gym."

Carmen asked, "I suppose you sanitized it."

The doctor answered, as though it were a ridiculous question. "Yes, of course."

"I'd like to check your cleaning procedures, if you don't mind," she requested.

"I'll get you in touch with the head of our cleaning crew," offered the doctor, reluctantly, not normally given to flagrant requests by outsiders.

"How much do you normally pay on complaints such as these?" Jeff asked, looking up at Larson.

The captain said, "Worldwide, it depends on the country that owns the ship." Pointing to the stack of folders, he added, "In these instances, it's the equivalent of 50-100 thousand dollars. One of them went for a quarter million. The couple had a good attorney. But you have to understand this goes on all the time; payouts, I mean. This ship nets two million dollars a week on items sold like souvenirs, jewelry and clothing, along with auctions, certain performances, contests, gambling, special classes, drinks at dinner, room moves, and a score of extras. We can't afford not to have these people stay quiet, especially when they have a legitimate complaint."

Late the following afternoon, the ship pulled into the Port of Seattle to spend the night. Disembarkation would occur by 8:00 the next morning with boarding at 2:00 in the afternoon.

Once the rain had ceased, Jeff and Carmen made their way down the elevator to the I-95 corridor, the main corridor of any cruise ship, and the only one where a person could see from one end of the vessel to another. Along the corridor were crews' quarters and their own exercise facilities, numerous prep kitchens, and storage for extra luggage. After the lengthy walk they reached one of the gangways. The tide had come in, so they walked downward to reach the land. In the afternoon, the situation would be reversed.

"Space Needle first," Carmen declared, making their way through a sea of bodies all headed for their designated locations, although it was not unusual for hundreds of people to stay aboard the vessel during a stop for a variety of reasons.

"Seafood for lunch," Jeff responded. "There's a place I read about online we must try." He fully expected prices to be jacked up, as is normally the case when tourist ships roll in, especially when two others were already docked ahead of them and another on the horizon.

Boarding a bus that had signage reading SPACE NEEDLE, the pair relaxed during the short drive to their destination. Jeff wanted to walk through the Science Fiction and Fantasy Museum Hall of Fame, which was part of the Museum of Pop Culture located adjacent to the Needle. Carmen had no interest in science fiction, whatsoever. Jeff needed the visit. He wanted to get himself thinking outside the box and what better way to do it than to leave the planet entirely, although some would say that Jeff's social problems arose because he thought outside the box more than he thought inside of it.

On the bus ride, Jeff pulled out his phone. Carmen expressed her annoyance. "Why are you playing with that? You know I hate it when we're out somewhere."

"Texting someone. I won't play with it after this," Jeff retorted, sharply, totally absorbed in the activity and somewhat annoyed at having his concentration broken. Once he had completed the task, a pang of guilt swept over him. Taking hold of Carmen's hand, he said gently, "Sorry, honey, I didn't mean to speak so gruffly."

A product of the 1962 World's Fair, the citizens of the city voted to retain the earthquake-proof 605-foot tall Space Needle as a public landmark. It bragged a 360 degree observation deck which could be reached after a four minute elevator ride. The landmark served to attract visitors from around the world.

Bypassing the tourist trinkets, the couple rode the elevator to the observation area to enjoy a spectacular view of the city, including the view of their own ship.

Jeff's phone vibrated in his pocket. He quietly left Carmen engrossed in using a built-in telescope, and walked to another area where he surreptitiously glanced at the text, punching in a few words to send, then quietly returning to her side.

From the needle, the couple traveled to Chilulu Gardens, named after Dale Chilulu, famed sculpture of enlarged spectacular displays of glass to awe the imagination. This is what Jeff sought—a challenge to the imagination. How each exhibit was carefully packed and crated and the expense involved in shipping the display around the world was open to the imagination.

Mindful of the time and after touring the gardens, the pair took a bus ride to Pike Place Market, and finally relaxed for a seafood lunch seated outside on a wharf. The choppy waves were blocked by the rise and fall of the bouncing ships in the harbor to provide the sound of gentle wash against the pylons and the shore. Mount Rainier jutted its 14,000 foot snow-capped peak 60 miles to the north.

On the table in front of them stood three pails: One filled with lobster tails and crab legs, another with bottles of beer in ice, and a third for trash. Numerous deconstruction tools stood at the ready for their use.

Looking out over the water, their ship in sight, Carmen wiped a morsel of food from the corner of her mouth with a napkin and asked, "Who was texting you?"

Caught by surprise, Jeff had to smile. With Carmen, honesty is the best policy. "Returning a text," that's all.

"No, that's not all. From whom?" she inquired. For an instant, she thought she might go into the field of dentistry considering all the teeth she had to pull to get Jeff of open up.

Once Jeff told her, she mumbled, "That's what I thought."

Back on track, speaking softly, he chose another subject. "What did you find out from the cleaning crew?"

Carmen answered, frankly. "They were thorough. I don't think either of us could have done a better job. I did take a lot of photos of the gym. Crew members have their own gym, but the complaints came from guests, not from crew members."

"Do you think they might have gotten something similar to Legionnaires disease from the saunas," Jeff asked. "Coughing was one of the symptoms."

"Maybe," she replied, "except that only two of them used a sauna after their workouts. Gastric upset was also a complaint, but that could be from overeating, symptoms of allergy, various infections, medications, psycho-somatic complaints, a lot of things."

"Any common machines they preferred?" he said, continuing with the interrogation.

"Elliptical, bikes, treadmills, floor mats for stretching, everything in my photos. I tried different perspectives with the pictures, but couldn't come up with any new revelations."

"How about the floor mats? I know these people don't have the materials and facilities to pursue the relationship between bacteria or even viruses with floor mat and humans, but do they sterilize them?

"They're sterilized on all sides daily," she responded.

"You reviewed their list of medications. Did anything stand out?" he inquired, trying to take all the bits and pieces and see if a picture emerged.

"Nothing in common. What I saw was a fairly normal distribution of doctor-prescribed meds stuff. Some of them never took anything except for aspirin and the usual OTC stuff."

"That's all good news," Jeff concluded, grinning.

"How so?" she asked, with narrowed eyes.

"It limits our options. That said, let's still get back and take a close look at your gym photos," Jeff replied. He added, "I'll connect your phone to our laptop for a better picture. There may be something obvious everyone is missing. Also, we didn't ask about any slot machines used or other gambling devices. These folks may be sensitive to a particular bug that the rest of us don't respond to. It happens all the time. Plus, hand-to-mouth transfer plays an absolutely critical role in COVID-19 transmission, as it does with flu and colds. At some time, we need to go over the medical records again."

Carmen had become tired of it all. Damn it, they were on vacation. She looked Jeff in the eye and accused, "Instead of trying to work all the time on this cruise, maybe we can have some fun, too"

"This is fun," he answered, without thinking. Reflecting on his reply, he thought: What was it he'd overheard someone say about him during a gossip session? *"Shenero's a high-risk-hi-gain person. His mouth gets him into trouble. But you can put your money on him. I mean, he'll stick his neck out there as far as he can and the son of a bitch will bite the man who's holding the sword at his head."*

Jeff recovered immediately and said, "Next stop Ketchikan in a couple of days. How about if you pick a performance you like tonight and take me along on a date?" Jeff offered.

"All right, deal. I also get to choose what we do afterward, too," she teased.

Jeff agreed. They both needed more intimate time together.

Three

The review of the photos proved fruitless. Just to ensure they had covered the bases, they visited the gym itself with no new revelations. To Jeff, that meant more good news because it eliminated another piece. He tried to work a puzzle in reverse: There was the outline of a picture in front of him, but he couldn't see it clearly because there were too many distractions, too many pieces piled on top of it. He needed to eliminate as many pieces as possible.

To Jeff's delight, the doctor could shed no light on the gambling habits of the complainants and LaMonde could offer nothing of assistance regarding their eating habits. It wasn't an absolute in either case, but the information helped. Two more pieces gone.

All the cases hinged on symptoms common to asthma and allergy, including headaches and gastric upset resulting in loss of sleep, possibly caused by excessive mucous drainage. These were not uncommon symptoms aboard a new environment, such as ship, with passengers wearing various colognes and perfumes in crowded venues, but deep coughs were a step beyond the common complaints. None were smokers, or at least had no recent record of smoking. Unfortunately, the limited facilities aboard ship obviated the ability to isolate bacteria such as pathogenic staph or strep. Even lung volumes couldn't be ascertained, which might reveal information about bronchiole irritation. Frustrated, Jeff wondered how one can reach a destination while flying blind?

Both he and Carmen were out of ideas and gave up the effort in order to temporarily to enjoy the cruise. Resting the mind allows the brain to sort through the trash and reorganize. Spending more time on deck at the rail, washed by a cold wind, they soon saw dolphins cavorting alongside the ship, keeping pace, diving, and jumping, showing off for the throngs lined up along the individual balconies at every level like different colored birds lined up on lines of wires, one above the other.

Ice floes began to appear in the colder waters, carried down from the glaciers melting in the northernmost climes of the planet. In Jeff's view, the Earth was going through one of its normal geological warming periods. Man happens to be here during the change and is taking credit for it. He occasionally wondered if the human race would survive its own ego, or end up like the sponge, a life form that dead-ended at the far tip of the multi-branched evolutionary tree.

A loud speaker announced that the blue color in the floes was an indication of intense pressure that had been put upon the ice at one time to convert it into a form of water not seen elsewhere. The announcer then asked the audience to look off to the northwest where the occasional streamlined body of a blue whale could be seen spouting, shooting water over thirty feet in height.

Amidst it all, the announcer said, "Will Doctor Jeffrey Shenero please call the central office." Jeff and Carmen wondered about a possible problem. Might there be an urgent message from the lab at home, an accident perhaps, a tragedy? If so, there was nothing they could do about it at the moment.

Jeff quickly located a red deck-side phone and made the call, spoke briefly, then hung up. "The doctor wants us," he said, feeling both relieved and confused.

 Rise to Eminence

"No, he wants you," Carmen replied. "I'm staying here."

The announcement rubbed Carmen the wrong way. It should have requested Mr. and Mrs. Shenero. Not for the first time she wondered why Jeff hadn't ever asked her to marry him after all they had gone through together and all the love they espoused for one another. They lived together, worked together and breathed the same air. The answer was obvious. Jeff was a coward; she knew it, he knew it, and he knew she knew it, which was a place he didn't want to visit.

That announcement would change their lives, because whether Jeff liked it or not, she would marry him this trip by the ship's captain, come hell or high water. Jeff had no problem getting married once. Never mind his wife left him for a real life, one that didn't get her embarrassed because of her husband's eccentricities and his big mouth. Carmen could be as stubborn and resolute as her partner. So far, that's all he was, a partner. She wondered if she served as a convenient person of interest to Jeff or if he had true love for her. Never mind hot passionate love. She wanted commitment.

The infirmary was located on the lower deck with services available 24/7, but these were limited to everyday problems, not surgeries or dental procedures. For those, the patient would have to wait until the ship reached the next port. Typically, non-surgical procedures include emergency cardiovascular care and minor procedures. The medical staff are trained and prepared to deal with influenza and GI issues, such as occurs during a norovirus outbreak. They can offer pharmaceutical advice for medications, such as for motion sickness. They carry backboards for spine immobilization, and some lab capabilities, oxygen, EKG, defibrillators, cardiac monitors and vital sign indicators. For them, it was a simple matter to recognize another complaint identical to those of concern and about which Dr. Shenero had been paged.

Jerry Richards had come from New Jersey. A computer engineer in his mid-forties, he stood a little less than six-feet in height and in need of some exercise, but had a clean look about him. Conversational and conservative, Richards opted for an interior lower priced stateroom. This was his first sea cruise. He began noticing the cough the second day of the voyage. It had worsened and he complained of nasal congestion and difficulty in breathing. Yes, he had been to the gym for a light workout and, no, he had not incurred motion sickness or eaten any food that did not agree with him.

The doctor and Jeff interviewed Richards, taking notes and pictures and creating a file. He said yes and no at the appropriate times, and in the end, confirmed a case similar to the others. His eyes watered, he had intermittent cough with inflammation of the nasal passages. The medical offices could screen for drugs and international regulations called for zero tolerance among crew members. They found no issues with Richards' blood after he readily gave consent to have it tested. Once the file had been compiled, Jeff recorded each page. When he reported the meeting to Carmen, she asked, coldly, still miffed at being left out of the meeting, "What now?"

"We get ready to play in the small town of Ketchikan that is snowed in for nine months of the year until the cruise ships hit port. Then sell, sell, sell and shop till you drop," Jeff quipped, sensing her mood and trying to make light of the present circumstances.

Ketchikan wasn't part of the Alaskan mainland, but belonged to a portion of the state that flowed down the western edge of Canada like an amoeba extending a pseudopod in search of food. It belonged to the Inside Passage, as it was called. The city brags a population of little over 8000. The average high temperature is approximately 50 degrees Fahrenheit and the air is always wet from either snow or rain. Ketchikan sells a lot of jewelry and leather goods when the ships come in, enough so that the citizens can buy sufficient supplies to hole up for another long winter. As the story goes, one annoyed tourist stopped a youth on the street and asked him if it always rained there. The youth replied that he didn't know about always because he was only sixteen.

Cafes ran the gamut from Chinese and Mexican dishes, to fish and burgers. Carmen watched Jeff eat an elk burger and down a beer and he watched her eat Chinese dishes and drink tea. Afterward, the couple took a short bus ride to watch a lumberjack show where the men, and occasional women, throw axes at targets, chop logs, and climb trees, before returning to the ship. They hoped the disease had not spread to other vessels. What's bad for one can be bad for them all.

Late that night, the couple sat on their balcony looking out at the moonlight reflected off chucks of blue ice and the sea itself. They sat quietly for several minutes, each wearing a windbreaker and wrapped in a blanket. Over her mood, Carmen said, "I suppose it makes sense if we accept our subjects all had a rare disorder that got triggered onboard ship."

"True," Jeff agreed. "Ships like these have been around for a long time. Okay, they've gotten larger, but why all of a sudden on this line?"

"And the patients come from all walks of life," added Carmen. "We've got a retired elementary school teacher, an attorney, a young couple on their honeymoon, a door-to-door salesman . . . mostly from different parts of the country."

"Let's talk about Juneau, instead. That's coming up next," Jeff said.

"I'm hungry," Carmen interjected.

"What? Do you know what time it is?" Jeff queried.

"And?" she asked.

An hour later, full of cake and ice cream, the weary couple hit the sack planning to sleep in. Unfortunately, it didn't work out that way.

At 3:00 am, Jeff's cell phone lit up and chimed, indicating a call was coming in through the ship's

WiFi system. The name read Emily Kaufman.

"What is it?" Carmen muttered.

"It's Emily Kaufman?"

"Who?" asked Carmen. "Oh, wait. Remember she got married a couple of months ago and said they had a quiet wedding, but she'd fill us in later and you wished her the best.

"That's right." Jeff mumbled, rubbing his face and texted back that she could call him if she wanted. Computing the time difference, he thought it must be around 6:00 am in Boston.

Within a minute, Emily did call. "Doctor Shenero, how is your vacation?" she inquired, to break the ice. "I called your office yesterday and they told me you were on a cruise."

"Smooth as silk," he replied. "Having a great time. How's married life?"

Emily briefly told him about how she and Arnold were meant for each other and then said, "Doctor, we're in the lab confirming results, but I'm certain we have a breakthrough. I mean, it was totally accidental, but I guess that's the nature of breakthroughs, isn't it."

"This must be serious because you're starting to ramble," Jeff said. He heard Arnold's voice in the background urging her to tell him.

"Yes, yes," she said. "Doctor, it's about the toxin produced by *Jeffrus shenerii.* Well, it does a lot more than we thought it did. You know how when we get a new toxin we test it against anything we can get our hands on, from bacteria, to protozoa, to plants and mice and even sea life. Well, a number of our people have small boats in slips in Boston harbor and one guy brought in a glass jar with barnacles covered with Zebra mussels that he scraped from the bottom of his boat. You know what zebra mussels are, right?"

Jeff scratched his head and saw Carmen propped up on her pillow, her hair looking as though she'd stuck her finger into an electrical socket. "No," he admitted, hoping this conversation was going somewhere fast.

"You don't?" Emily announced. "Zebra mussels are the scourge of the seaways. They grow on anything, rocks, metal, even other life forms like barnacles, such as in our harbor here and in Seattle and the Mississippi, and so forth. They're destroying the natural ecosystems at an incredible rate. The barnacles themselves are dying because they can't get food. The mussels extrude this protein-foot that allows them to stick onto things. It turns out our toxin causes the protein to release its hold because the mussel thinks the amino acid phenylalanine tag that's on the toxin is its own phenylalanine and incorporates it instead, which causes it to release its attachment. Doctor, all we have to do is to come with a way to apply this to patches of zebra mussels and we can save a harbor and a zillion ships. "

Jeff finally grasped what Emily was telling him and asked, "But obviously the same toxin will kill other life forms."

"No, not at all. That's the beauty. The toxin

degrades in salt water within a short time and disappears entirely after doing its dirty work on the mussels."

"Emily, the Mississippi River is fresh water," Jeff argued.

"Only the top portion," she countered. "The bottom is lower than the gulf, so salty sea water comes in and layers along the bottom. It's not perfect and we have a lot of work to do, but we feel good about it."

Like any good researcher, Jeff knew that a moment of excitement in a lab is a merely a brief flash of light in a long dark period of drudgery. Still, he had to admit, Emily was onto something and he latched onto her excitement. "Emily, I want you and Arnold to send me what you've got and, for what it's worth, I'll look at the data. I know you have an army of good minds out there, but I'll be there for you both, if you need me."

"You will? I was hoping you would say that. It would mean the world to me . . . to us, doctor. There's another thing too," Emily quickly inserted. "When we prepare nutrient agar with 1% petroleum distillate added, the mold grows rapidly and it produces spores. They have an odd bronze-like appearance, almost umbrella-like and appear in long chains that easily separate when exposed to the slightest breeze. We'll forward the pictures to you. Anyway, say 'hi' to Carmen for us.

"Say hello to her yourself, Emily," Carmen said, taking the phone from Jeff's hand.

Carmen spent a half hour talking science with Emily and then with Kaufman, roaming charges be damned. When she closed the call, she found Jeff sound asleep laying on his stomach. Staring at him, the thought about how much she loved him. She thought about the meaning of their years together. She had sacrificed her medical degree to be with him.

She made a final decision. They would be married on this voyage. The man was like the magician on stage they had seen the other night, a man who puts up a good front to slither out from a trap, always making a successful escape. Read: Jeff Shenero, marriage escape artist.

Carmen returned to bed and half-slept, smiling, thinking, finally coming up with a plan of action, careful not to force an event only to be sorry later. With Jeff as the subject, that might be a legitimate concern.

Four

Before whale-watching, taking a helicopter ride to see Mendenhall Glacier and going dogsledding in Juneau, Carmen thought she might add a little real excitement to Jeff's life by taking him jewelry shopping aboard ship before hitting port. Nothing serious, just something to eat away at his mind during shore leave.

The overly bright main promenade could have been a small shopping mall anywhere; a ring of small stores stocked with books, souvenirs, dresses, sunglasses, deck wear, athletic equipment, handbags, cell phones, and, of course, jewelry. No fast food restaurants here with too many free food options available. This one had a 5000 square foot supervised play room for children with everything from slides for toddlers to wall climbing for teens.

Leaving the souvenir store, Carmen meandered toward the area where a number of people were looking into the showcases of fine jewelry. She winked at the young sales girl as they approached. Jeff, who had been inclined to head toward sporting goods, failed to notice the sales girl wink back.

Carmen parked herself in front of the case with rings, saw one she had noted on a previous visit, and said to the girl, "Could I take a closer look at that one, please?"

"Of course." The girl reached into the showcase to remove the diamond ring Carmen pointed to.

"Mind if try it on?" Carmen asked the girl, who looked to be in her mid-twenties, unmarried, and eager to please.

She had Jeff's attention.

"Absolutely," the girl said. "We can even size it for you and have it ready by the time you leave the cruise. Our experts are the best."

Carmen slid the ring on her wedding finger and held it up for Jeff to see. "What do you think, honey, isn't it gorgeous?"

"Uh, yeah, it does look good on you," he replied, his discomfort evident.

"It's is a little loose, though," Carmen said to the

sales girl. She removed the ring and made a show of looking at the price tag attached to the ring. Holding it up to Jeff, she said, "Definitely affordable, don't you think, sweetheart?"

"You're not thinking . . . ," he began.

"What if I am?" Carmen asked.

"Uh, maybe we should talk about this later," Jeff offered, blushing somewhat.

"You bet we will. But before that, we need to look at the men's rings."

Carmen handed the diamond ring back to the smiling girl, evidently enjoying herself, and doubtless would pass on the story in short order. Carmen led Jeff to another section of the showcase where she, more than he, looked at men's wedding bands.

Minutes later, they headed toward the door leading to the deck where she quickly found a couple of lounge chairs for them to call their own and talk about something he had no desire to discuss.

Five seconds after they put on their lightweight nylon windbreakers and relaxed in the breeze of the moving ship, Carmen said, "They're called wedding rings, Jeff."

"I know what they're called," he retorted.

"And?"

"And what?"

"Are you that naïve?" she queried, beginning to get upset again.

"Are you asking me to marry you?" he asked.

"No, stupid, I'm asking you to ask me. Mother of

God, help me with this idiot," she said in Spanish.

"Carmen, maybe I'm not ready . . . , " he began.

"Well, you know, Jeff, it's been nice." At that, she got up and walked away. This was as good a time as any for her to grab a few things and head to the library for an all-night reading session before hitting Juneau in the morning. Jeff could do what he wanted.

At 3:26 am, Jeff found asleep and in the library with a book in her lap. He stroked her hair to gently waken her and said, sheepishly, "If you like that ring, then it's yours, although I think we can do better than that when we get home."

"That one will be fine, dear," Carmen smiled, sweetly, not giving him any wiggle room.

"I'll set it up with the captain tomorrow, after we hit port," Jeff replied. "Now I need to get a little sleep. This is a big ship. Looking for you took some time."

The wedding took place in the ship's chapel, shortly after departing Juneau. Jeff invited LaMonde to be his best man and knowing no one else, Carmen invited the sales girl who had sold her the ring to be her witness. Delighted to receive the invitation, the girl accepted the offer, believing it to be a good omen for her.

That evening the couple sat at the captain's table as his guests. At the beginning of the dinner, Larson stood and addressed the other diners, all of whom were dressed for an elegant dinner. He toasted the newlyweds who stood and raised their glasses in salutory congratulations, then returned to the meal.

In the morning, the ship reached Glacier Bay National Park and stopped for a period of time to watch a glacier calve, and the wildlife, which included the humpback whale, harbor porpoise, harbor seal, sea lion and sea otter. Bird watchers with binoculars and checklists made frequent shouts of discoveries of some 260 species of birds inhabiting the bay. After a full day of stoppage, the boat moved on toward Sitka, a Tlingit Indian name for Baranof Island.

The couple cavorted on their own for five hours in the small community, visiting the art galleries and absorbing the Russian heritage of the city. They returned to their stateroom, tired from hours of walking, to find a letter slipped beneath the door. Picking it up, Jeff closed the door, took off his woolen cap and sat at the edge of the bed. Carmen sat next to him. The envelope had the name *Dr. Shenero* handwritten on it.

Opening the envelope, Jeff pulled out the folded paper fax received by the ship two hours before. It read:

Dr. Shenero: This missive is in response to your short cover letter and the ten files you sent to our office via phone. Our investigators have found that most of the people described are members of an extended family and there is a possibility that this is a scam. Included in this group is the one person onboard ship whose file you also sent. Unfortunately, there may be other possibilities for the complaints, such as similar genetic sensitivities, and until we have more information, we cannot proceed further. Any assistance you can give us will be appreciated.

Signed,
William Butler
Washington, D.C. Bureau Chief
Federal Bureau of Investigation
601 4th St NW, Washington, DC 20535

Jeff flopped back onto the bed. "Thought so," he muttered. "We can't ask security to interrogate the man. He'd just deny it and raise a stink."

"Once we get underway, the next stop is Vancouver Island and that won't be for a few days. Maybe by then we might be able to make some headway on this case," Carmen offered.

"Here's an idea," Jeff said. "How about if I do call security. The captain already told us to mention his name if we needed anything at all in this matter. Everybody's returning from Sitka so they can have one of their people keep an eye on Richards' room and let us know when he gets in."

Carmen caught up with the story. "I already turned in my ring to be sized, so I'm single again. I go down and knock on his door by accident and ask him if he could he show me what's what."

"'What's what' can have a lot of meanings," Jeff teased.

Carmen ignored him and continued, "We become friends and start to hang out. He wouldn't have seen me at the big wedding dinner because that was above his pay grade. I'll mention his cough to him and at some point I might get him to confide in me about how he got it."

"Perfect. Your Spanish accent adds flavor to the pie. Do you think he'd feel less threatened if you let him know you have money?" Jeff asked.

"Let me think about it. I may have to play that one by ear," she replied.

"What if he already saw us together in Sitka? It could be a problem," Jeff said.

"I don't see why? I have a right to make friends onboard, don't I?" Carmen grinned. This could be fun.

A half-hour later Jeff got the call that Richards had returned. Carmen took a quick shower, remained in her jeans and sneakers, but changed into a low-cut see-through blouse with black bra. She ran a brush through her hair, put it on beneath a red scarf, adding some deep red lipstick, and a dot of perfume.

Carmen walked the distance to the elevator wondering what the hell she was doing and how this whole thing started. It began when Jeff probably saved a girl's life, and the father, Pierre LaMonde, rewarded him with a free cruise as a reward. Or maybe the father thought Jeff would be helpful in solving the health issue that threatened his job and used the daughter as a perfect excuse to contact him? Did it matter? Jeff could have handled this on his own. Now she finds herself prepping to hit up a stranger on her honeymoon. Welcome to Sheneroville.

No, wrong thinking. She felt compelled to help her husband in any way she could, just like had helped her, including bailing her out of jail years before. Call it sharing lives.

Richards' cabin was located several levels below theirs toward the middle-rear of the ship. In modern ships, the interior decks are usually numbered from the primary deck, which is #1. Richards was housed in cabin #A4-24, or, three levels above the primary deck plus his room number.

The erstwhile porter saw Carmen coming and nodded at the door to confirm it to be the right one, then moved on. Other guests were returning from the land excursion at the same time going into their respective units, many bearing small souvenirs.

Carmen walked up to the door, as though it belonged to a close friend, and knocked. Within seconds, Richards opened it. Game On.

Five

"Oh, hi," Carmen said, in heavily accented Spanish, "I'm sorry, I must have the wrong room. I got a room number from someone and thought I could remember it. I'm all turned around. I don't know where I am, Could you show me . . . how do you say, 'what's what'?"

Two hours later, Carmen returned, having gone to the ladies room once to use the ships' WiFi system to text Jeff. She informed him that she and Jerry were getting to know one another. She had only a single drink of wine to his two vodka martinis.

When she returned, she reported to Jeff that she had told Richards she thought he had an interesting childhood, traveling with his military family, but didn't want to catch whatever he had that made him cough. Richards had told her it wasn't contagious. She had asked him how he knew and he said he just did. They set another date for the next night.

On the second date, Carmen and Jerry ate a late dinner at a family-style restaurant featuring fried chicken, pot roast, lamb chops, mashed potatoes, steamed vegetables, lentils, and weineschnitzel paired with sauerkraut, for the German-minded patron.

After dinner, Jerry guided Carmen to his side of the ship to revisit the same club next to a large capacity theater that played a different movie each night.

The couple found a table away from the band playing slow jazz. Ella Fitzgerald and Louis Armstrong look-alikes were performing "Sing a Little Song for Me." The hour embraced a late night crowd with perhaps 80 patrons occupying the venue.

After Jerry ordered two vodka martinis, Carmen warned, "Jerry, I have something to confess. I'm a lightweight drinker, so watch that I don't drink too much, all right? It's a genetic thing. At that she took a strong pull on her drink, set it down, and pretended to push it away with her hand.

"Will do, Carmen," Jerry replied, amused by her antics. "You were telling me about an abusive husband last night. It sounded like it's in the past. Is it?"

Carmen had given Jerry her first name to avoid confusion later. "I'll drink to that," she said, enjoying her lapse into heavily accented Spanish, as the raised her glass. "The *pinche cabron* was into drugs, too. I hope you don't do any."

"Never," Richards admitted. "Alcohol is fine with me." His cough had disappeared for the evening and his eyes were clear, although, with her medical-eyes, Carmen observed that the upper portion of his nose had a slight swelling, as though he had been snorting cocaine or got popped in the nose with a fist.

Jerry spent some time telling her about himself, explaining about how to build better computers and programming them. Carmen tried to keep her focus and pretended interest. Electronics was not one her specialties.

Jeff had learned that Jerry Richards had another doctor's appointment the next afternoon, so Carmen put the squeeze on him. He couldn't go into the medical office free of symptoms, but he had to stay that way to lure Carmen. He had no choice but to continue with the act, if that's what it was. What he might be up to was probably a lot more important than scoring with her.

When Jerry did visit the doctor on schedule, his symptoms had returned in full and hadn't cleared by the time Carmen came to his cabin only three hours later for their third date. When he opened the door, dressed for a evening out, he spoke nasally and coughed after every few words. When Carmen saw that she said, "Jerry, you told me you didn't do drugs and look at you. I need to go."

She turned to leave and Richards gently took hold of her arm. "Wait, please, let's go down for a few drinks first and talk, then you can go if you want."

Carmen humphed, "Next thing I know you're going to start beating me, probably because I'm rich and live in a penthouse suite in First Class and you're a substance abuser."

"Please, just for a few minutes, Carmen, give me a chance to explain," the man implored.

Carmen hesitated before replying, "All right, just for a few minutes but if I think you're doing drugs, it's over."

The couple ate dinner again then returned to the usual nightclub. Carmen used the swizzle stick to stir her half-finished third drink and began to giggle. "Oh, Jerry, you can be so much fun. By the way, what did the doctor say about your problem? Come on. You said you'd tell me."

Jerry said, nonchalantly, "He thought it might be an allergy and gave me some anti-histamines. He said it should clear up once I left the ship. See, nothing complicated."

"Oh, honey, that such good news," Carmen slurred, leaning forward in her low cut blouse, her cleavage serving as a powerful eye magnet. "I'll tell you a big secret of mine, if you tell me one of yours.

I can guarantee I'll never remember anything you tell me, anyway, by tomorrow morning. My friends say I'm brainless. She thought, *Careful, Carmen, don't overplay your hand.*

Carmen appeared to make an effort to put together the next words. "Jerr, hon, that's one of my secrets. You want to know another one? I like bold men. And maybe someday I'll tell you how I got my money because I got stories to tell."

She knew the drink was getting to her when she thought that maybe she should have taken the offers to be a cover-magazine model, the new wife of a famous scientist and a national hero. A movie or TV contract might follow. She had the urge to slap herself back into reality as she saw the grin on Jerry's face, as though he were making headway with this gorgeous creature.

"Gee, you were supposed to tell me your secret first," she concluded, and downed the rest of her martini, gently sucking on the olive with red, pouted lips, starring goggle-eyed at the man across the table from her.

Jerry settled back in his seat assessing the situation, tossed down the rest of his drink, ordered two more, and leaned toward Carmen. "Powdered white chili peppers," he said at last. "You inhale them. They get absorbed and none of it can be detected because nobody looks for that. But they cause a lot of symptoms that make the doctors all go crazy. You can measure the symptoms, but not the cause. In the end, the cruise line always pays. I can tell you that for a fact."

Carmen shook her head, slowly, swaying it, her eyes unfocused from the vodka. She understood it all, but she had passed her drinking limit. In her enthusiasm to be a spy, she failed to order a glass of water to drink alternately with the alcohol.

Feeling secure in his conquest of this jewel of a wealthy woman who clearly ached to take him to bed, he said, "Money, honey. Look at the billions these people have. They can spare a few dollars once in a while."

Carmen laughed out loud and leaned forward again toward the grinning man to be as intimate as the table would allow, noting where Jerry's eyes went. The noise of the band caused her to shift from a seat opposite Jerry to a seat next to him. She leaned in a couple of inches from his face to ensure he received a little whiff of baby powder fragrance. She need to reaffirm his statement. "I get it, Jerry. You pretend to be sick and stick them for money later in a lawsuit. You have to keep it up for a while after you leave, right?"

"No, I am sick, Carmen. I have a lot of relatives who got sick too. It's genetic," Jerry answered, toying with her, pulling her strings in different directions, telling but not showing.

Their drinks arrived. Sensing Jerry might be thinking about asking her back to his cabin, Carmen said, "Let's toast to Jerry's illness," and raised her glass. An instant later she set it down, swayed into him slightly, and said, "Oh, Jerr, I don't feel so well.

I'll be right back."

At that point, Carmen stood unsteadily, using the table for support. In point of fact, she didn't feel well. She had always been a lightweight drinker, preferring wine over anything else.

Fortunately, Jerry's back was to the club's entry, but as she stood up straight to leave, Jerry gently grabbed her arm and pulled her down to his face, whispering, "Honey, that's just pocket change. You ain't seen nothing yet."

He released her arm to let her go, then pulled out his phone to begin texting, not noticing Carmen walk out the door of the club, thinking she needed the ladies' room. Once outside in the circle of stores and using the ship's WiFi, she texted Jeff: ONMYWAY. Somewhat unsteadily, she grabbed the nearest elevator, thankful to be the lone occupant.

After a slow ride, she exited the elevator to find she had pushed the wrong button and had gotten off one floor too early, according to the signage. The door closed behind her and not trusting herself to take the stairs, she punched the button and waited. Within a few seconds, the elevator stopped at her floor and the door opened. A middle-aged couple dressed for the evening stood in front of her. "Going down?" the man asked, holding open the door.

"Going up, actually," Carmen responded.

"Sorry," said the man, who let go of the door.

Carmen listened to the elevator stop on the three more times before reaching the bottom. Now, she really did have to pee. She looked at the stairway again, a declined its invitation a second time.

At last the door opened and the rode it the single floor to her level. She carefully negotiated the corridor to their stateroom, trying not to bounce from wall to wall in a hallway not much wider than the width of a wheelchair. When one did come through, a person coming from the other direction would have to step into a small alcove in front of a cabin doorway to enable it to pass.

Carmen's mind swirled with bits of conversation, then returned to thoughts of herself. She realized what she had done, what she had become. This was all completely out of character for her. She was a dutiful educated office manager, investigator, scientist, married woman, and a lot of other things. But within the past couple of days she had found a new role for herself as a manipulative, deceitful person. To make matters worse, she felt good about it, comfortable in the role, as though it were completely natural for her to act in that manner. Is this the new Carmen? She hoped not.

She found the door unlocked to see Jeff seated at a small writing table working on his laptop. He turned toward her as she entered, anxious to hear her tale worthy of a soap opera. "I was getting worried," he said. "What took you so long?"

"Elevator troubles," Carmen said, throwing down her small purse on the bed. She unbuttoned her blouse and reached down inside her bra to pull out the miniature microphone blue-toothed to the hidden tape recorder inside the waistband of her jeans. Then she entered the bathroom to return a short while later, greatly relieved.

"All right, let's see if we got it. I'd hate to have to do it again," Carmen slurred.

Jeff came over and put his arm around her. He said, "Baby, you overdid it. Sit down."

"I'm tired of sitting," Carmen declared. Rewinding the message, she played the last portion, but stopped the recording at the end of the confession, which came out loud and clear.

"Damn you're good," Jeff said, giving her shoulders a squeeze and kissing her on the cheek. "The problem is, I don't think there's anything solid here. He mentioned everything from allergies to pepper to genetics, but let's get this to security, then we'll tell Captain Larson and LaMonde. I'll let Butler over at FBI know, as soon as I can get to the message center.

Carmen went to the bathroom to wash her face and drink a glass of water. When she returned, she did sit on the bed and said, "It's just one partial admission. It doesn't directly implicate the others."

Jeff added, "True, if there were he might rat on the others. Too bad security can't check his person or his luggage. It's a great idea, the pepper thing, though. It makes sense to me. What do you think?"

"I think poor Jerry will spend the rest of his life wondering about how Carmen fit into all this," she concluded, her mouth downcast in a mock show of sadness, her head spinning. She needed to fix the problem.

"After we take care of business, I could use a drink," Jeff suggested to lighten the mood.

"Not for me, thanks," Carmen replied. "I think I'll lay off the stuff for a few days. All it does is make a person talk too much."

At that, they both laughed. Comedy relief in a tragedy. Carmen finished putting herself back together, looking forward to some late night coffee, bed, and a good night's sleep. She would definitely ensure that cell phones and ringers would be turned off. With her husband around, anything was possible.

"I'll have a pot of coffee brought up," Jeff offered.

Fifteen minutes later the couple sat on the veranda outside their suite looking out at a bright crescent moon hanging over the water. Occasional lights shined from land in the distance. The cold air helped to clear Carmen's head. She held a large hot cup of mocha coffee in both hands sipping it slowly, emotionally drained, recounting the evening. Something nagged at her.

"In the morning, we need to listen to everything," she said.

"Over two hours?" Jeff inquired, very certain he didn't want to hear about how Jerry grew up while listening to Carmen cooing over his every word.

Carmen shook her head and said, "Not really. Since the recorder is voice activated, it shouldn't be that long. There's something he said that's bothering me and the more I think about it the farther away it runs," she confessed.

Back in their room, Carmen played the recording

of her evening with Jerry. She let it play until after the confession and after a slight pause, she announced she didn't feel well and Jerry had replied, "Honey, that's just pocket change. You ain't seen nothing yet."

"Play the last part again," said Jeff.

She did as he requested. They could have saved a lot of time by simply listening to the last five seconds.

The ultimate conspiracy theorist, Jeff could take a good molehill and turn it into a very bad mountain, but somehow it worked out for him. He said, "Jerry's playing a role like you are. This Jerry guy is not all he seems. Something very bad is going to happen. If we give that confession to the authorities and call it a day, that won't be the end of it. Even under pressure, there's a good chance this guy is not going to turn in the others. He's too hard core."

"What do we do, nothing?" Carmen asked, her eyelids getting heavy.

"You're going to need to see him again," Jeff suggested.

Carmen sat bolt upright. "Oh, no. That is so not going to happen," she declared with certainty.

"I'm going to call security, identify myself, and ask if they have the capability of capturing fingerprints, then we can go to sleep," Jeff suggested. Without waiting for Carmen to reply, he made the call.

Six

Reluctantly, Carmen knocked on the door, but got no reply. On a hunch, she went to the nightclub she and Jerry frequented and surreptitiously looked in to see him seated with another woman at the same table they had used. Both had drinks and finger snacks in front of them. Appraising the woman, Carmen saw her to be a little past middle-aged, handsome, well-constructed and wearing a modest dress that didn't show much except for neck and upper chest. Her well-styled brunette hair came to her shoulders. Both appeared to be enjoying themselves.

Carmen felt relieved and frustrated at the same time. To interrupt them would create an unpleasant situation. She feld relieved not to have to deal with having to explain herself to Jerry, yet she wanted to get it over with. She allowed the night belonged to him and would try to see him again the next evening. On an impulse, she pulled out Jeff's cell phone he gave her for a backup. It had three cameras and an excellent zoom feature. She focused on the couple while trying to look like a tourist taking pictures, at the same time patiently waiting for Jerry to around for a good picture of him, as well.

Why wait until tomorrow evening, she told herself. She'd knock on his door late morning, say, before lunch, and presumably, if this woman had been his date for the night, she would be gone by then. He might be, too. It's worth a try.

She found Jeff in the gym finishing a workout and told him what had happened. He agreed to her idea of her trying to see him earlier the next day and within a half-hour, the newlyweds went to the dining room for a casual dinner and chilly roof top stroll in the park. The park consisted of a bar and grill, enough seating to accommodate hundreds, a pool, and a forested areas with hundreds, if not thousands of plant species awaiting those who appreciated walking through vegetation from around the world.

Despite the relaxing stroll, Carmen slept poorly that night thinking about various possible conversations she might have with Jerry the next day, working out responses to his questions in detail, like anybody working hard on a project at hand.

A little after 10:00 am, almost robotically from lack of sleep, Carmen went down to Jerry's cabin and knocked on the door. He had either gone or didn't want to open the door. So much for all night deliberations. She met Jeff in the library where they browsed through the books, then went to the gym, ate lunch, and tried to kill time by going to the movies. Neither of them could enjoy the film.

Once, Jeff looked at a new watch he had acquired and punched the face to scroll past the oxygen monitor, the EKG sleep memory graph, the heart rate monitor, stop watch, countdown timer, alarm, jogging and step counter, altimeter, barometer, GPS, compass, phone message center, and music stations, but he never could find the time, so he pulled out his cell only to get admonished by nearby patrons.

At 6:00 that evening, Carmen made a second try, thinking that neighbors must wonder who she was, as if it mattered. When Jerry did open the door, he stood shirtless, wearing jeans, with a towel in his hand. Before he could say a word, Carmen said, "Sorry, Jerry, I came by to apologize."

"Come in," he said, sweeping his arm inward, coughing slightly.

He must have visited the doctor again to go on record, Carmen thought. She had suspected Jerry had a good frame with his clothes on. With his shirt off, she thought that a year of hard working out could transform his body into something admirable, although not to her. He could never work out enough to equal her husbands' rock-hard body. She also noticed the bed had been made, so no evidence there of any recent activities.

While Jerry slipped on a pullover, Carmen began, "Jerry, I don't even remember going to bed. All I remembered in the morning is that we had a good time talking. I'm sorry I didn't come back."

Struggling for words, she added, "I told you I couldn't hold my liquor. Besides . . . well, this is embarrassing, but, I have . . . female problems I had to take care of."

"You mean like an infection?" Jerry grinned.

Carmen laughed. "Yeah," she said.

"Till how long?" Jerry inquired.

"I don't know. It flared up this trip, but the ship's doctor only gave me OTC stuff to take. Big deal. I need something stronger. Anyway, I came by last night, but I guess you were out."

"To tell you the truth, I went out looking for you,

but I guess you were holed up somewhere," Jerry divulged.

Carmen thought. *Liar. Maybe he doesn't want to admit he went out on you, which means you can't trust him. Just like he can't trust you. Forget it. I need to get him to tell the truth.*

"You don't remember anything about the other night?" Jerry asked, combing his hair in the mirror. If he had plans to go out somewhere for the evening, this could delay her own plans even further.

Carmen shook her head. She had let her black hair down and the ringlets danced across her shoulder blades. "I had this sense that we talked about a lot of money, at least I think so, but I can't get there. It's gone. I like alcohol, but it doesn't like me."

Fully expecting him to reject her offer, she plunged into the deep end. "Anyway, if you're open for a little while and don't have somewhere to go, maybe I can treat you this time."

"Only if you promise not to run away again," Jerry said, with a sparkle in his eyes.

"Deal," Carmen agreed.

On the walk, Jerry added to the list of jokes he had been telling her by saying: "Three engineers are on their way to a convention when their car stalls. The mechanical engineer says, 'I have my tools in the trunk. I can fix it'. The electrical engineer says, 'I have my multimeter with me, I can diagnose the problem', and the software engineer says, 'Nothing complicated. Let's get out of the car and get back in. Everything will be fine then'."

Carmen didn't think the joke very funny, but she laughed out of politeness. "Cute, Jerry, I'll try to remember that," she said, occasionally chuckling, as though the more she thought about it, the funnier it became. She had heard ribald versions of the same story that were quite humorous, the memory of which actually did provide the mirth required for the occasion.

By her third drink, Carmen faired better than on the previous occasion by sipping wine, alternating with sips of water when Jerry asked, "What's it like up there in first class with the wealthy."

"How did you know I'm there?" Carmen seemed genuinely puzzled.

"You told me when you yelled at me," Jerry laughed. "You also said you'd tell me how you got your money."

"I did?" Carmen slurred. Looking around, she left her seat opposite him and took the chair to his right, leaning toward him whispered, breathing alcohol on him, "You won't tell?"

"Promise."

"I told you my husband was into drugs. Well, he flew for the cartels. He never stole from them, but over the years they paid him millions in honest hard-earned dollars. I knew where he stashed it and it wasn't in a bank. Millions, Jerry. All the money belonged to him and when his plane crashed, it became all mine."

"Where was that?" Jerry inquired.

"Guadalahara, Mexico, where I grew up,"

Carmen replied. *And went to medical school,* she didn't add.

Suspiciously, Jerry said, "I know Guadalahara. Have you ever eaten at La Chata on C. Manual Cotilla?"

Carmen smiled, "Silly, you're confusing that with Restaurante Allium, the open air restaurant on that same street right next door to the nightclub Villa Acapulco."

Carmen had passed the test. Still, Jerry wanted to find out more about her. "Besides Mexico and the U.S., where else have you ever traveled to?" he asked.

"That's all," she answered truthfully.

"Because over the past ten years I've spent time in Russia, France, England, and various countries in South America. My business allows me to travel."

"What kind of business are you in?" Carmen inquired.

"Selling advanced shortcut software that allows you to save time," Jerry said.

Carmen shook her head, not understanding, but at least he was warming up.

At that point, Jerry repeated what he had told her about his money-making scheme. Carmen resisted the temptation to place a hand on his inner thigh, something she enjoyed doing with Jeff; in fact, her heart began racing at the thought. She quickly realized there is more than one way to have sex and she wanted none of it with him. She needed to stick with the program. Taking another sip, larger this time, she gave him a light kiss and replied, "To most people, that's a lot of money, but in the grand scheme of things . . . "

"Nah, that's lunch money. Here's the real deal. You hack into the cruise ship's computer system that controls the money flow and direct it elsewhere."

"Oh, is that all," Carmen quipped. "You're a computer guy, why don't you do it yourself? Here you are settling for chump change like thousands when you can have hundreds of millions or billions."

"Honey, I'm a shopper, not a doer. Besides, chump change can add up. Look, any computer system can be hacked. We . . . I need a very good hacker for the job. It costs money to make money. Hacking is like medicine, real estate, law, or construction. You can't know it all so you pick a specialty. If you want to turn off the lights of a city, you go to one kind of guy. If you want to steal credit card data from Walmart, you get another guy. All of the targets have common codes, but also specific codes. I needed to find somebody who worked with codes similar to those used by cruise lines and line them up to work in my specific area. Does that make sense?"

"Sort of," Carmen admitted. She picked up on his usage of the word *needed.* Did that mean the job is over? She also admitted to herself that it may not make sense to a layperson such as herself, but an expert might be able to get something of it.

Jerry continued, "The people I have lined up are specialists in this area. They've done it before. They also travel a lot internationally for obvious reasons.

They'll immediately confiscate 25% of the take, but want a million up front. It's almost there. I need to raise capital. Most of it has been accumulated fairly easily over the past couple of years. That's the bare bones I'm going to tell you."

"If they're that good, why do they need you at all?" Carmen asked.

"Because I know pass codes and short cuts. They need me and I'm not good enough to do it by myself. I'd leave my electronic fingerprints all over the place. It's simpler to pay somebody else to do it. These guys won't leave a trace, except for something that might smell Russian and that's par for the course, these days."

Carmen had to be careful of entrapment, although, actually, he had opened the door. She took another drink, sat back in her chair and slurred, "I'm going to make you an offer, but first I want a selfie with you."

Without waiting for a reply, Carmen reached into her clutch and pulled out her phone by the edge and handed it to Jerry. He took it from her, suspicion clouding his face. Carmen said, "What's the matter, Jerry, afraid I'm going to make an eight-by-ten of it and hang it on my wall?"

Carmen could see him process the request. Handing the device back to her, he said, "Sorry, I never did like pictures of myself."

Distracting him she said, "Guess I'll just have to remember you," taking the phone by the edge and replacing it, trying not to smudge any prints.

Now the hard businesswoman, Carmen said, "I like to invest in people, but frankly, Jerry, I'd loan you the money for a piece of the pie, but I don't think you have anything to give me for collateral."

"Will the title to my Lamborghini serve as collateral?" Jerry offered, a big grin crossing his face.

Fully prepared to accept that the man had nothing but bluster to back up his words, Carmen was taken aback at his statement. "And you just happen to have that with you," she stated, flatly.

"Correct. I don't have liquid cash and that's what some people want," he replied. He pulled out his wallet and slid out a laminated photograph of a yellow Lamborghini Urus and another with a photo of the title with his name on it.

"I'm impressed, Jerry. What's it worth?" Carmen asked.

"It's a year old and worth about $150 K. Look it up. Obviously, it's paid for because the title is in my name. I also carry the real paper with me for deals like these. I always come through with my end of the deal because I still have the car."

"How much do you need?" she asked

"I need 100 K."

"It'll go nicely next to my Porche 911 Carrera," Carmen said.

Jerry laughed. "Nice thought, but you'll never get it. You'll have your money back in a month."

"With 15% interest," Carmen threw in.

"With interest," Jerry said.

Carmen leaned back and nodded up and down with large slow motions. She turned down her mouth as a show of understanding and said, "Tell you what, we'll talk details in two days right here. That'll give me time to move some money around, that is, if you're interested in a bank transfer."

"Are you going to remember anything about this in the morning?" he queried.

Carmen replied, "If I drink lots of coffee, I'll be fine. I have my own medical problems to deal with, so I'm going to try to get some rest."

She left early, rightly trusting that Jerry's mind had shifted from sex to serious financial matters. Once in the cabin, she replayed the conversation, and, as they had done the first time, Jeff recorded it onto his cell phone for backup, leaving hers alone.

Again, Jeff said, "Nothing solid, again. For all we know the entire family suffers from some genetic problem, got paid because they picked up some unidentified infection onboard ship and contributed the money to Jerry for his scheme to hire the hackers. Yes, they're contributing to a criminal enterprise, but it doesn't yell scam to start with. Does that make sense?"

"My head hurts," Carmen responded.

Captain Larson had said he would make himself available to them and, as the hour was still early, the couple met him at his personal communication center along with the head of security, a well-constructed man with a crew haircut by the name of John McKenzie, a retired naval officer. A lone white-shirted technician worked at the various screens when they entered the room.

Most cruise ships cost from half-a-billion to a billion dollars to construct. One this size costs a lot more. None are lacking in communication equipment. Anybody with sensitivity to EMF radiation would be advised not to enter the room packed with electronics, radar screens, satellite connections, WiFi, Internet, ship security systems including cameras, meteorological data, and basic phone lines to everywhere in the ship.

Carmen carefully removed the phone, almost pouring her purse onto a table, tying to keep her makeup in the handbag at the same time. McKenzie reached into a briefcase and pulled out a roll of 2-inch wide clear Sellotape and tore off a portion at the seam. He then carefully placed it over the phone, pressed it in place and peeled it off. Fingerprints were clearly visible on the tape, which then got placed onto another piece of clear tape and put in a bag on which he wrote identification numbers. He did the same thing for the other side. He then asked Carmen to press her fingers and thumbs of both hands onto other pieces of Sellotape which he also labeled. He handed all envelopes to the operator.

McKenzie said, "Go ahead and send me that picture, ma'am."

"I have several on this other camera. Some with Jerry and some with the other woman he met," she offered.

"Send them to Captain Larson's computer,

please," McKenzie requested. "And, the recording device, if you don't mind," he added, holding out his hand. He received the device and turned it over to the operating technician.

McKenzie said, "There is no emergency on any of this because we'll have to work with authorities to build a case. I'll turn in the evidence in person once we reach port in San Diego. In the meantime, Captain Larson will work with your husband and Mr. Ortiz to send what you just gave us to our people and to your husband's contacts."

Jeff said, "Question. Does she have to meet this guy to hear more details of his plan and try to close the deal, or do you have enough to prosecute?"

McKenzie said, "Prosecution is not in my realm, and honestly it's all hearsay without solid evidence. It would be nice to find out who this Russian hacker is."

Larson said to the couple, "I'll leave that decision up to you two. You've both done admirable jobs."

Jeff felt great respect for Carmen. She had gone the extra mile. Enough. Even if these hot shot hackers were caught, more would move in to fill the vacuum. All the evidence pointed to bailing out. He said to Larson, "Tell you what, let's send what we have and get that off the table. It'll probably take them a week or more to put anything together and by that time we'll be back home."

Ortiz looked up at Larson who nodded and said, "What's the number, Jeff?"

Jeff told him and Ortiz made the call. The answer

came on speaker. Jeff identified himself, provided the necessary passwords and asked for William Butler. He turned to the others and said, "Butler is the head of the FBI's Washington D.C. field office."

A talking head appeared on screen. The head possessed razor cut gray hair. He could have been the neighborhood banker who slept well with less bags under his eyes than a neighborhood banker. "Yes, Dr. Shenero. Nice to hear from you. What information do you have for us today?"

Jeff said, "We're going to send over some pictures, fingerprints, and electronic recordings that directly relate to the shipboard scams we spoke of earlier." He explained about his presence on a ship and the people accompanying him, introduced Carmen, who had done all the hard work, then asked Butler for the bureau's fax number.

"Great. We'll watch for them," Butler replied, then provided the number.

Ortiz looked up at Larson who gave the nod and Ortiz went to work.

With that, Jeff and Carmen went to the outside railing to shiver in the cold air of an overcast day with their arms wrapped around each other ready to return to their vacation. Case closed.

Seven

At approximately 11:15 two mornings later, a call came over the ship's speaker: "Will Dr. and Mrs. Jeffrey Shenero please call Extension 264."

Of the thirty people attending the auction of

paintings ranging from $50 to several hundred dollars and more, two of them rose and left the room.

In the corridor, Jeff said, "That number belongs to the security line."

Carmen grinned, "I'll get it this time."

Jeff followed her to a red wall phone. She picked up, spoke and listened, then hung up. "McKenzie wants us back in the communications center."

"That's interesting. I wonder if it has anything to do with our landing in Vancouver in a couple of hours," Jeff said.

A different white-shirted technician with the name of Woolridge on a name tag sat at one bank of instruments when the pair arrived minutes later. Larson and McKenzie were also present.

Butler is on hold for you," Larson said, with a dour look, as though a bomb threat had been called in.

Butler's face came on the screen. He said, "We have some information for you. We processed all the data you sent us and . . . "

Jeff was amazed and couldn't stop the short nerve that connected his brain to his mouth. "Already?" he interrupted.

Butler smiled, "Yes, Jeff. Despite what you may believe about the slow movement of government, there are times when we can make things happen very quickly. Jerry Richards is as he seems, at least according to what we can find, or not find. He's traveled to the countries he said he traveled to, lived in each of them for a period of time, and he has no criminal record.

"The woman he was with, however, is a different story. Captain Larson told us she came onboard as a married woman with the name of Sandra White. Her husband is named William White. We don't have a picture of him, but we've got a 95% match of her through the use of facial recognition technology—great close-ups, by the way, Carmen. Her true name is Marina Sobol, a Ukranian. She's vying for top honors on Interpol's list of bad girls. We have no record of her being married. She's strongly suspected of being part of schemes for fraud and computer hacking on a grand scale, an arm of a larger network, actually, that is bringing chaos to Western countries, including our own."

Carmen voiced all their concerns, when she asked, "Which means she and Richards knew each other before the trip. But if she's the hacker, why is she onboard at all?"

"That's what we're trying to work out," Butler said.

Larson asked, "We're going to need to arrest them before we dock in Puerto Vallarta, unless you have other plans for surveillance."

Carmen stared at the screen as though she were in a trance, exclaiming, "It wasn't on the recording, but it was something Pierre LaMonde, the Executive Chef, told us during our first meeting. He told us that cruise ships bring in an incredible amount of money each week for sales of souvenirs, books, clothing, and money spent on a wide variety of activities that don't come with their ticket. Could that be part of what they're up to?"

Jeff gave a slight grimace. "But there's no cash. If there were, I should think he would hire a safe cracker, not a computer expert."

A voice could be heard on Butler's end. The bureau chief turned his head to speak with another man, whose face appeared on the screen. He identified himself as their resident computer technician. "Thank you for that—Carmen, is it? The way I see it, they can't do what they're planning from the land, simply because they have to tie into the onboard ship's computer that transfers the credit card money to the central bank. In layman's terms, if you ride the express train to the bank, you end up inside the vault and you can make your transfers outward from there. "

Jeff queried, "Then why did Richards even tell anything to Carmen, other than to maybe hit on her?"

"Maybe because he still needed cash to speed up the process," Carmen conjectured.

McKenzie said, "Apparently not, because Marina and her maybe husband and Richards had all made arrangements for the trip some time ago. That's why they're all here together."

Everyone was silent until Jeff snapped his fingers and said, "Trial run. Marina and hubby needed to check out the system, but Richards wasn't giving them everything they needed to get completely in. He still owed them money, but was close enough to making full payment that Marina and hubby came onboard to check out what they would have to deal with later.

"Maybe Richards was supposed to come up with it all in a certain period of time or lose it all. Maybe she had other jobs lined up in the queue, so she put the squeeze on Richards for a final payment. This caused Richards to entice Carmen to put up her money."

McKenzie suggested, "They may wait for another cruise to pull it off because time is getting short. Richards is nervous. He's afraid Marina is going to walk. He doesn't want to wait months for the cruise lines to pay him for his soon-to-be medical claims. At this point in the game, he could lose the big stash they're all after, plus make a lot of relatives very angry that they invested in him and lost their hard-earned money."

Carmen said, "With my bank transfer he can close the deal."

Jeff suggested, "If he's confident you'll give him the money, I'll bet no bad guys are going ashore in the interest of time and they're going to work in somebody's room. There are still days of sailing before we reach home port."

Butler offered, "If we grab Marina and Richards, the husband will probably disappear in Vancouver. I'm going to send her picture along with Richards' to my people there to surveil them, if they do come ashore. The hallway cameras can tell us when they leave. We don't want to move too early or we might lose him. These people are very slippery and they're always on the lookout, but somehow she has to report to her reputed husband. And just because she meets somebody at all doesn't mean it's him, or even if he's a bad guy.

"Captain Larson, I'd like you to delay your departure if necessary until we have completed the arrests."

Larson said, "I'll be happy to comply, but you should have plenty of time because we don't depart for at least two hours after boarding has been completed for a number of reasons. Once of them relates to excursions that run overtime."

Butler said, "I'd like you to watch both rooms. When we board, we'll see if Jeff is right. If nobody leaves, we'll make our move."

On an impulse, Jeff asked, "Captain, where is Marina's cabin located?"

Larson looked at McKenzie, who checked his tablet. "She's in A4-23."

"What?" Carmen exclaimed. She could not contain her surprise. "That's next door to Richards'."

McKenzie checked further and said, with great concern, "Correct, there is an adjoining door connecting the suites, which means they must have requested this when they signed up for the cruise."

Larson said, "Mr. Woolridge, please shut down all credit card and electronic transfers. Don't make a general announcement. If complaints are made, provide our apologies and tell them our systems are under repair until further notice."

Not having seen anyone leave either Jerry or Marina's room after the ship reached port in Vancouver, Carmen knocked on the door of A4-24, waited a half-minute and then knocked again. Maybe nobody was home. Preparing to knock a third time, Jerry opened the door only slightly, saw her and said, "What, Carmen?"

"Sorry to disturb you, Jerry. We came into Vancouver a few minutes ago and I wanted to know if you'd like to keep me company. We can talk business. The money's ready to transfer," Carmen said, contritely.

"Can't. I'm going to stay here. I don't feel well, okay?" Jerry insisted, making a move to close the door.

"Don't you want to close the deal?" she continued, pressing him.

"I said I'm busy. Maybe tomorrow," Jerry repeated, forcing the door closed. She heard the dead bolt click into place.

Carmen smiled for the hall camera and walked away. Before she reached the end of the corridor, she had to make way for three suited men coming in the opposite direction.

Eight

Returning from their Vancouver tour, the couple were in good spirits until they began coughing. They hadn't been in their stateroom more than a couple of minutes when Jim McKenzie summoned them to the security office. Captain Larson was busy making preparations to get the ship underway and couldn't attend the meeting.

McKenzie's office had been a stateroom turned into a work center without an outside view, basically in the center of the ship. It held file cabinets and two desks, two computers, printers, and storage for various security devices. The other members of the security staff were housed elsewhere. McKenzie asked them to find an available seat and relax.

McKenzie said, "The two foreign hackers aren't saying a single thing, but Jerry Richards told us a lot. First, he saw Carmen right away as somebody from the insurance company who was trying to entrap him, so he told her the entire story about the pepper, trusting she would believe it, but would have absolutely have no proof. He teased her with the truth. In a word, she was too good to be true.

"We went through Richards' possessions and couldn't find the pepper or anything at all that could be used, as Richards had described in the recording. He admitted to the wire fraud because we caught him red-handed, but as for the other, he laughed it off. He admitted that his relatives were involved in a plot to hire the hackers, but in this case, the disease is real and he wants to file suit. You are not the only ones on your level to have episodes of coughing with eyes tearing. Can you add anything to this, Carmen?"

She said, "The disease does seem to be real and it appears to be communicable, despite what Richards told me, which makes no sense from an epidemiological point of view. You can expect a disease to spread outward from a point source, but I was the only one Richards associated with who lived on the upper level, at least as far as I know. Was I a carrier? Did this disease have a short incubation period of only a few days then everybody got hit at the same time? And, given he thought I was trying to entrap him, why did he even tell me about the hackers, unless he really did need the money? Honestly, we're confused. Being human, we think the worst, like something similar to norovirus."

She did not have to mention what everybody present already knew. The fast moving virus caused hundreds of passengers to fall ill on Royal Caribbean's Oasis of the Seas in January 2019. And according to what LaMonde had told them during their day with him, three Carnival cruise liners, all refurbished in 2019, were being parted out on muddy beaches of Western Turkey at a loss to the company of well over four billion dollars.

Taking a standing position over the two seated guests, McKenzie said, "The captain wants to keep this outbreak under the radar as long as we can, but this thing can explode at any minute."

The role of the head of security onboard ships is not easy. He deals with numerous incidents such as drugs, missing persons, sudden deaths, a vast number of accidents, thefts, deception, and rape. He has to write numerous weekly reports and the crew has to be constantly on their toes due to a host of random cabin searches on a weekly basis. They would also be subject to monthly random drug and alcohol testing in an atmosphere of zero-tolerance. All of this would be set aside if epidemic-related issues occurred, because of time constraints.

At that moment, McKenzie received a call. He listened and closed the call. Rubbing his forehead, he said, "We have a client in a cabin at the southeast end of the ship, where there is more sway—as do all corners—who has a friend in a luxury suite who is complaining of coughing. The client took this to mean that her own back hurt when she got up the morning, so she filed a complaint. This means I have to take the time to prepare a report."

This suggested to Jeff that events had escalated to another level. Reality is what it is, but a poisonous snake can have a lot of fangs. He could make the case that most of our beliefs are based on rumor, not fact. He could lecture ad infinitum about it. People accept rumors more readily than truth, unless the truth teller can be completely trusted, and even he or she can have the facts wrong.

Listening to McKenzie, his mind began to wander. Somehow, the ship's air conditioning system had to be involved. He brought up the subject and McKenzie said, "I already spoke to several of the ship's engineers. They said there is no way to contain an outbreak like norovirus, or COVID-19, or influenza, because even if you quarantined people, the air conditioning system would recycle the air and send it to other areas of the ship tied to the infected cabins."

Jeff saw this as the missing piece because the

air handling system serving the upper level of the ship was independent from the others because it recycled its own air and mixed it with fresh air. This knowledge gave him a measure of confidence that the disease wouldn't spread throughout the entire boat. It did not eliminate the possibility of their infecting people on other levels, either directly or indirectly through the use of fomites. Yet, that didn't happen. Therefore, they were dealing with either a non-communicable disease, or one with some, as yet, undefined incubation period.

Something came to Jeff's mind during his ruminations and out of nowhere he asked, "John, can we visit the engine room?"

Becoming accustomed to Jeff's occasionally erratic behavior, McKenzie led them to a particular elevator and inserted a key, then pushed a button marked #3, which meant two decks below the primary deck, or on this ship, some 20 feet above the bottom of the hull. On level #3, they walked along a long corridor with a number of doors on both sides. He led them into one of them and found an older man named Barney, a 30-year veteran of the shipping industry, who wore a hardhat and carried a clipboard.

McKenzie said, 'Barney, these folks want to see the ducting for A-8."

Barney replied, 'Okay, it's over there." Leading them, Barney started to walk and explained, 'Working these boats is like driving the first Model T car compared with what's out there today. They all got wheels and doors and an engine, and that's where the similarity ends. These big babies carry 2 million gallons of fuel and you need special training just to understand how to read the gauges."

He led them to the air handling system that fed the uppermost deck when Jeff asked, "Can you show me the filter, please?"

"Sure," Barney said, and opened a horizontal door, pointing to the HEPA filter. Jeff had his suspicions and requested, "Can you pull it out without touching it?'"

Barney shrugged, walked away, and returned with a pair of channel locks, which he used to grab the filter and slide it out about six inches. There in the grooves of the pleated filter stood small mounds of powdered white pepper.

"Kind of thought that might be the case. Can you please get a large plastic bag and put the filter into it for evidence?"

Turning to McKenzie, Jeff said, "There's your epidemic on the upper deck. See if you can get any prints off the leading edge. Richards had to pull it out to put the pepper on it."

"Good call, Jeff," Carmen squeezed his arm.

McKenzie asked Barney, "Nobody can just come in here, can they?'"

Barney said, "Of course not. However, yesterday morning we did have our usual walk-through of the mechanical room for passengers who were interested."

Within the hour, McKenzie had taken prints

from the leading edge of the filter and had sent them to Butler at FBI who confirmed them to belong to Richards, matching the ones on the cell phone. Once the source of the problem was eliminated, the problem soon disappeared.

Takeover

The long cruise down to Mexico gave the Sheneros time to relax and unwind from their adventures, which were unbeknownst to the other passengers. It gave them time to go to the movies, watch various performances, enjoys the auctions and try different restaurants. At this point, it seemed as though nothing else could go wrong.

Except for an occasional assassination, the city of Puerto Vallarta, located in the western state of Jalisco, is deemed safe for tourists. There exists an ample number of police armed with pistols, rifles, and submachine guns to watch over tourists. This, plus a training facility for the federal police only a few miles from the beachfront helps keep the drug lords from overrunning the city, as occurred in Acapulco when hotel occupancy dropped to record lows. Some 200 miles to the east, the city of Guadalahara is also a favorite site for tourists and a plane stop for those traveling farther south or farther north. The state also boasts vast acreages of sugar cane and its processing plants.

Numerous cruise ships can be seen in Puerto Vallarta throughout the primary tourist season. This stretches from November into April or May when the temperature remains fairly stable between 85-90 degrees Fahrenheit during the day. This is perfect weather to eat shrimp ceviche and grilled red snapper while sipping on a Corona beer followed by smoking a Cuban cigar at a seaside cafe. Once late spring and early summer come about, the humidity increases and monsoon season begins, replete with hurricanes.

Jalisco is also home to the New Generation Cartel, one of the most ruthless drug cartels in the country and second only to the infamous Sinaloa Cartel, with designs to more heavily infiltrate Central and South America, as well as northward to dramatically increase activity into the United States and Canada.

The Cartels' main cash flow is drug trafficking, with secondary income sources coming from arms sales, hostage negotiations, and other sundry practices. Buying off police departments and entire governments is well within their capabilities. They are favored by many small communities because they pave roads and occasionally construct needed edifices. However, terrorism, per se, does not rank high on their list of activities for various reasons.

This was about to change when one of their newly hired terrorist geniuses devised and presented a plan to take over an entire cruise ship with some 10,000 passengers and crew members. He quietly proclaimed that he wanted to be like Yasser Arafat, founder of the PLO, who had originated the art of hijacking commercial aircraft and mid-air bombings. He died a billionaire.

The original plan would take some two years to actualize. It did not include the presence of cartel members for the primary reason they were not skilled enough to carry out the concept with the efficiency required for this world-class operation. It would be both intricate, yet clean and simple at the same time. Every person must be hand-picked and educated. To do otherwise would involve unnecessary risks. This matter met with resistance. Cartel members must play a major role in the project. Call it an ego thing. Call it a trust thing. That's how they operate.

Aboard these cruise ships, and once in port, the gangway watchman, appointed by the chief of security—in this case John McKenzie—has several functions: controlling access to the ship, controlling people and equipment to and from the vessel, searching personnel and/or baggage, if necessary, and reporting security incidents or breaches. He also has overreach to inspect incoming cargo and passengers for unwanted additions, such as weapons and explosive devices.

In case of emergency, the international SSAS, or Ship Security Alert System is triggered during a serious threat of any kind, including attacks by terrorists, such as occasionally occurs off the coast of Somalia, an area notorious for ship hijackings. From the watchman's signal over his walky-talky, this beacon transmits to the local authorities, the company security officer, and the naval operations center sponsoring the ship resulting in the dispatch of the military, as well as hostage negotiators.

Aside from freighters, the good news is that the control cabin of the ship is secure at all times. The bad news is that, for this plan to work, it didn't matter. While always alert for armed intruders coming up the gangway, there is no way to tell if onboard passengers are a potential threat.

In terms of financial gain, it would make no sense to hijack an empty ship and hold it hostage. Blow it up and they'll build another. However, when the ship is full of passengers, this presents a different picture in the eyes of the world. History has shown that individuals or governments will pay for hostages a million dollars each, even though they publically announce they will pay nothing. If 10,000 hostages and a two billion dollar cruise ship is at stake, the ante is considerably higher.

Billions of dollars in ransom money would catapult the Jalisco cartel onto the world stage. It would give them enough cash to recruit anybody anytime and would enable them to sweep across northern Mexico and totally take over the United States, not only in terms of absolutely flooding every corner of the country with narcotics through totally porous borders, but in terms of buying off everybody they damned well pleased to pay. Either that, or eliminate those who stood in their way. Call it business as usual.

If entry by armed persons were attempted, the doors to the ship would be immediately closed, and authorities notified. Therefore, entry would have to occur toward the end of the boarding period to maximize the number of hostages on the ship, which meant, for the takeover to be successful, several factors would have to come into play. Mercenaries would have to be imbedded as part of the passenger cluster, and armed men and women would have to board the vessel. They need to be the same people.

Once the gangways had lowered, the main I-95 corridor began to fill with passengers awaiting the disembark announcement. A series of announcements did occur admonishing the travelers to follow standard safety precautions by not straying too far from the beaten path, protecting their valuables, paying attention to return time, taking note of the bus they were on, and so forth.

These operations typically went smoothly and so, when the doors were opened, the crowds moved leisurely down the gangways in no particular hurry. At the bottom, Jeff and Carmen moved along with a knot of passengers being directed by numerous personnel to available taxis and buses. The latter ranged from 12 to 92 passengers. In their instance, they climbed aboard a bus that held some 25 people; Bus No. 8. The couple found themselves in the middle of the pack and during the shuffling for seats, a middle-aged man wearing a white panama hat stepped on Jeff's toes. Turning to Jeff, he said, "Pardon," with a French accent. (Because the tour originated in San Diego, most of those aboard spoke to each other in English or Spanish-accented English, one couple spoke French, and another couple spoke German.)

"No problem," Jeff replied, smiling.

A minute later, the driver stood up and announced that he, Enrique, welcomed everyone to Puerto Vallarta. He announced, with great enthusiasm, "This is Bus No. 8. Be sure to come back to this bus at 3:00 pm. Now, I want everyone to say 'hi' to everyone else, and let's have some fun!"

His enthusiasm became infectious and, after passengers had done as requested, Enrique closed the doors and began the drive from the port to the beach.

Some passengers opted to take boat rides to nearby islands or to shop in port-side stores, while many chose to remain onboard to enjoy the solitude of an empty ship. Four of those remaining would assist in other, more nefarious activities during the boarding process in the afternoon. Indeed, some ten members of the Sheneros' bus party would later go into the backrooms of certain stores for reasons of their own.

After 9:00 am, when the buses did unload, Jeff and Carmen grabbed a taxi to take them a few miles south to a 14-tier zip-line in a jungle area where the movie Predator was filmed. They recognized a young couple from their bus group and began small talk with them. Their last zip-line took them over a deep gorge and landed them at a ground level where taxis awaited and videos of their adventure could be purchased.

Returning to the city, the couple ate traditional Mexican food at a waterfront café and met two young newlyweds from New Jersey who were eating like they'd never tasted good Mexican food. Before them stood two 14-oz extra-strength margaritas. Jeff quietly told the waiter to add their tab onto his.

As they walked the stores amidst heavy tourist foot traffic, mostly from two other cruise ships in the port, hawkers tried to sell them everything from discount tickets for various events to Tee-shirts, to time shares. They marveled at the Huichol beaded art that challenged the imagination with its intricate designs. Some model animals, such as a life-size jaguar, were covered with a hundreds of thousands of beads of all colors laid onto a bed of beeswax. Prices varied from tens of dollars to several thousands, with shipping optional.

Following their examination of the Huichol art, the couple visited a number of stores all proudly displaying the Mexican fetish for silver, stores specializing in silver items of every ilk, from jewelry, picture frames, and serving sets, to ornately carved silverware. Finally, keeping an eye on the time, the couple walked the half-mile to the bus drop-off point.

People tend to take their original seats on a return trip. When boarding the designated bus for the return trip to the port, this did not occur, for the large part.

Jeff sat by the window in the same seat he had on the way out about mid-point in the bus, with Carmen seated next to him. Looking around, he leaned over to her and said, quietly, "This is Bus No. 8, right?"

"Yesss," she replied, elongating the word, wondering why he had asked the question.

"Well, if you look, you'll see our friends from Idaho we met in the gym the other day are not here yet. Most of the passengers are gabbing like they spent the day enjoying the city, but a few look stone-faced like they're riding a New York subway. Okay, no big deal, but why do we have a different driver. Something doesn't feel right. The guy who stepped on my foot isn't here, but somebody who looks like him is wearing his hat. We were all instructed to come back to the same bus for check-in purposes. I mean, the black haired woman who sat in the front row with the scarf must have let her hair grow inches longer over the last few hours."

Not understanding Jeff's point, Carmen casually looked around, as though gazing out the farther windows and thought Jeff might be playing a game. "Okay, we have some look-alikes, including pale skins, although I do see a few Hispanic looking types in the mix. Maybe aliens changed places with some of our people."

Ignoring his wife's statement, Jeff exhaled in exasperation. He stood up to walk up a few feet to the driver and asked, "Where's Enrique?"

"Who?" the driver asked.

"The other guy who drove us," Jeff answered.

"Oh, he got sick and they asked me to take his place," the driver said.

"Aren't we supposed to have the same passengers we had on the way in? Isn't that the rule?" Jeff persisted.

"I don't know anything. I just drive. Please take your seat," the driver replied, gruffly.

Jeff returned to his seat and repeated the conversation to Carmen who began to take her husband seriously. She looked around again, this time more boldly and patiently, examining faces. A few passengers saw her and turned away.

Turning her head back, she said in a cheerful voice, as though she might be relating a joke she had heard, "You're right, honey. This is too strange. I don't know what to make of it."

Jeff leaned forward to ask the man in front of him, who was not the same man who sat there on the way out, "Say, how did you like Sitka? Did you go on the train ride?"

"Yes, it was cold but great," he answered. Turning to the woman seated next to him he asked, "Don't you think so, honey?"

"Absolutely," she said, smiling.

When Jeff leaned back, Carmen whispered in his ear, "There was no train ride in Sitka."

"I know," Jeff muttered, simply.

"Got it. My turn," Carmen said. She leaned across the aisle, and, with a great smile worthy of a ditsy broad, chirped in Spanish to the nearest man, who differed from the man who had initially occupied the seat, "I'm from Guadalahara. My husband is from the United States. Is this your first tour? What part did you like best?"

Another man seated at the window next to the man she spoke to said something and her subject turned away to speak with him, instead.

If it looks like a fish and smells like a fish . . . Jeff thought, carefully watching the encounter. He texted McKenzie. JOHN: I AM ON BUS NO. 8. ON RIDE BACK WITH CARMEN. SEVERAL PASSENGERS APPEAR TO BE NEW, BUT ALL STILL HAVE SHIP BADGES AND COLORED WRIST BANDS FROM OUR BOAT. MANY LOOK-ALIKES FROM RIDE OUT TO PV BUT SEVERAL NEW HISPANCIS. NOT ALL SAME PEOPLE WE CAME OUT WITH. THEY AVOID SPEAKING WITH US. ALSO NEW DRIVER. WHAT TO DO?

When he hit SEND, he got a NO SERVICE message. Looking around he saw others on the bus trying to call or message out with no success. His active imagination took him to another scenario, which would be that the message did get through and a return text might read: GET OFF FIRST AND QUICKLY COME UP FIRST GANGWAY. SSAS AUTHORITIES NOTIFIED.

He would show the text to Carmen, who might smile as though one of their children had wished them well. At that point, Jeff would surmise that McKenzie had undoubtedly notified the other ships in port of an imminent threat. Or alternatively, that he had been killed and the gangsters had taken control of the vessel to make their demands known. A nightmare would ensue that would surely attract the attention of the entire world with him and his wife trapped in a ship of horrors.

Jeff was pulled back to reality when, over the loudspeaker, the new driver announced, "We will be delayed. We are waiting for other passengers."

Some 40 minutes later, the waited-for couple appeared, along with a single Hispanic woman, all contrite and apologizing to everyone for their tardiness. "I'll bet a couple of thousand people got on ahead of us," Jeff groused.

The fish he suspected began to stink. Somebody on the bus was using a cell phone jammer. Either that, or the terrorists had taken over the entire 4G/5G tower network.

Jeff directed, "Carmen, get up and take pictures of everyone in the bus like a happy camper wanting every memory of their vacation. I'll take video. Who's going to stop us?"

Again Jeff tried to text McKenzie with no success. His imagination led him to see a hostile armed takeover of the ship.

After they stopped at the port, two other buses arrived behind theirs. A crowd of men, women and children walked up the first gangway, slowed by a woman being pushed in a wheelchair.

"Let's take the far one, it's less occupied," Jeff said. "I don't think we're in any position to help John, right now."

Jeff mumbled, "This could be embarrassing. I sure hope we got his right, or I'll be crawling under a rock to hide."

"What do you mean 'we'?" Carmen declared, completely confused by the actions of her husband."I mean, talk to me. What's going on, honey?"

"I think we have a takeover by terrorists," he replied, grabbing her arm and marching her forward a rapid pace, yet trying not to display the concrn he felt.

"Jeff, where are we going?" Carmen inquired, deeply concerned, pulling her arm away.

"To see Larson and his crew on the ship's bridge. I'm afraid for McKenzie. I'll bet he and his friends are being held quitely under gunpoint and have been replaced. They're still letting passengers aboard. Come on."

"You and your conspiracy theories. Sometimes you make me crazy," Carmen shot, yanking her arm free from his grasp.

"Yeah? Think how I feel," Jeff retorted.

The couple walked along the crowd of passengers returning from their excursion, unsuspecting their ship could be on the verge of capture and they all might end up on the bottom of the ocean if things didn't go well.

"How do you know? I mean . . . ," she tried desperately to understand.

"Because it's the only thing that makes sense," he said.

In a few moments they had knocked on the door

of the bridge where Larson and several other crew members were preparing to get underway. Larson saw them at the door and let the couple enter. Jeff looked piqued, taking time to explain what he believed to be transpiring.

Larson looked from one to the other, while Jeff went through his explanations and bemused, looked at Carmen and asked, "Do you believe this?"

"Well, I'll admit it is a little extreme, but I know my husband . . ." she began.

Larson laughed. "Jeff, buses are not my specialty, ships are, but I'm a human being and I get on the wrong bus occasionally when I'm not driving this thing. People do it all the time on excursions. It's human to make mistakes. And there is never a good time for cell phone towers to quit working no matter where you are, expecially here in Mexico."

Jeff was adamant. "I think we got delayed on purpose and I think John is being held against his will right now."

Larson pursed his lips in a show of impatience and stated, "Dr. Shenero, I am fully aware of your eccentricities, if that is the right word, and your tendencies to exaggerate. However, I have a position of responsibility on this vessel. You don't. You're a passenger, who, I admit, has helped us greatly, both of you have, but at the present, your fantasies are becoming somewhat troublesome. Might I suggest you attend the theater or a show to lighten your moods?"

In a manner of perfect timing, an announcement came over the ship's intercom system which said, in perfect unaccented English, possibly with a suggestion of American Deep South accent. "Ladies and Gentlemen. My name is Charles and we are in control of your ship. We closed the doors and raised the gangways. You will eat dinner at the usual hour tonight, but from tomorrow on, you will be given a light breakfast and a single meal at night. I am instructing your executive chef, a . . ." here Charles paused, then said, "Mr. LaMonde, to work with the steward and their crew members to re-refrigerate unused food so it is not wasted. You may be onboard here for several weeks while we negotiate for your release.

"Your cell phones will not work because we control the towers in the city and will soon control the communication systems aboard the ship. Don't worry about your friends back home. They will soon know of your situation."

Larson looked at Jeff who shrugged in a "told you so" manner. It was obvious the attackers were making the call from the office of the cruise ship director, the person in charge of activities and announcements. He said as much, "They've taken over the director's office. They'll be here in good time."

Larson turned and said to Wentworth, who was following the conversation, "Activate the SSAS."

The couple were later to find out that Wentworth went by the nickname of RR, or Resident Robot. A balding middle-aged man, unmarried, with the personality of a rock, any crew member who knew him would trust him with their life.

Wentworth sat at the com screens, while another officer checked radar, GPS, and conducted other necessary functions related to a ship's movement. Larson ensured the door was locked behind them, not that a passcode lock would prevent the entry of an armed intruder, but it might slow him down. He thought for an instant, then changed the code from the inside.

Jeff said, "Mr. Wentworth, can you get me Mr. Butler over at FBI again, please? That is, with Captain Larson's permission."

Wentworth looked at Larson, who gave a sheepish okay, and in a few moments Jeff had explained what was occurring onboard and that he was sending videos and stills of the bus passengers, half of whom were probably terrorists. He would describe those he suspected.

Butler asked to speak with Larson who came over to the link. "Mr Larson, can you sail the ship back to your point origin in San Diego now?"

"That's what the schedule calls for. Nobody has pointed a gun in my face yet telling me to do otherwise," Larson replied.

Jeff had always wondered whether crime would be less if it were recorded, but not reported. Take two identical small cities, for example. In one of them, information is deliberately withheld from the press about muggings, shootings, breakins, rapes, holdups, carjackings, and other felonious crimes. In the second city, all are reported. In the end, would there be less crime in the non-reporting city?

To anyone within earshot, Jeff said, "My guess is these guys want to make their announcement to the world in their own way. That's why they shut down the towers. How about if Captain Larson disables all communications to the outside world, including the ship's WiFi, as well as their ability to make announcements to anyone. This would include among their own team once you shut down WiFi. The bad guys won't be able to speak to anyone to make their demands known, let alone be able to negotiate, or even to order the passengers around for whatever reason. Nobody in the outside world will know of their crime, let alone negotiate. If you do that, they'd be dead in the water with nobody to talk to except each other, or to commiserate with the passengers."

With Butler on-screen watching the exchange of ideas, Larson finally got with the program and suggested, "If they do get in here and order me to make contact with the outside world, I'll tell them it's a new company policy that everything gets shut down in case of a terrorist threat, which this is. Only corporate can turn communications back on, including transmission to satellites, so we couldn't contact them if we wanted to. In a manner of speaking, we're dead in the water, too, with only running lights, gambling, two meals a day, and San Diego to look forward to. There won't even be police on the ground here in Mexico trying to board the ship. If they did, they wouldn't know who to look for anyway. Can you make that work, Mr. Wentworth?"

"I can make it happen," Wentworth said. Did Jeff

detect a slight grin on the robot's face?

Carmen added, "Let's hope they don't have somebody who is knowledgeable about electronics. My guess is they don't, having had my experiences with them in Mexico. But times have changed. Anyway, when we reach San Diego in a couple of days, they'd have no option but to lower the gangways and order everyone off, while trying to get lost in the crowd with nothing to show for it."

Larsen stated, "Ten thousand against ten aren't good odds for them." He scratched his head and added, "I'm okay with the plan, but I'll need corporate's approval to shut down. Whatever we do, somehow the world will find out, it always does. There may be repercussions. Typically, the cruise lines like to communicate when there is a problem. This would be an entirely new approach."

"Let me take care of that part," Butler added. "We have to move hard and fast on this before you get a knock on the door." His image faded.

"Why aren't they here yet?" Carmen inquired.

"I think there's a fly in the ointment and it's probably ego," Jeff surmised. "Elements of this takeover smell less than class A-1, which is what you'd expect for an operation of this magnitude. Now that they have McKenzie and his people and had closed the doors and raised the gangways, they may figure they're home free, but to assume they can do what they want when they want at this point is foolish. Their game is communications and so far, they're playing minor league. Somebody on their side may very unhappy when this is over."

Carmen stared at her husband wondering how he could analyze a problem from outside the box when she needed to go step by careful step to reach a conclusion.

With the ship pulling out to sea, it took only minutes for Larson to get the go-ahead plan from corporate headquarters. Wentworth shut down all com systems using an emergency shut-off code to which only he and Larson were purview.

A knock on the glass caused Jeff to spin his head toward the entry door to see McKenzie standing outside, backlighted by the brightness of the late afternoon sunlight, trying to get in, but, according to his motions, couldn't get the passcode to work. Jeff took a couple of steps to the left for a better view and saw two men standing to the side of McKenzie. He had no doubt they were armed.

"Sven, John's got two men watching over him. What do you want to do?" Jeff asked.

Larson looked for himself, seemed to make a decision, then moved to unlock the door. When he did, McKenzie entered followed by the two men, one of whom was clearly Hispanic, rough looking, dressed darkly, no doubt their muscle. The second man was taller than Jeff, very pale skin, thin, light brown hair, dressed casually in a button down and blue jeans. Jeff didn't recognize him from either of the bus rides. He would be hard to miss. Perhaps he had remained on the ship the entire time.

The two men displayed handguns and the taller

one said, "We're taking control of this ship and your communications."

"Charles, how nice to meet you," Jeff said, as though greeting a long lost friend.

The darker man spoke to his partner in Spanish, while looking Carmen up and down, with a leer. Charles said, "From what I hear you're the two taking pictures on the bus."

Jeff responded, "Correct. Keepsakes of our vacation."

"And you're the man sitting across from me on the bus who didn't have the courtesy of answering my simple question. Where's your Latino courtesy?" Carmen said to the second man, in Spanish.

Both men looked somewhat taken aback from the words spoken from the couple and hadn't yet heard a word from somebody in charge. One of them said, "Yes, I'm Charles and I'll take your cell phones with our pictures, thank you."

Jeff and Carmen surrendered their phones. Once done, Jeff remarked, "Honey, now we don't have anything to take home to remember our vacation by."

"Enough," Charles said. Jeff saw the guns weren't aimed at Carmen, but both men were close enough to chance a couple of fast solid kicks to their lower sections and break some noses afterward. He decided to let events unfold.

"I'm presuming you're the captain," Charles said to Larson. "I want to make an announcement and you will open your com to me."

Larson said, without the slightest quaver in his voice, "I want to accommodate you, but my hands are tied. Let me educate you." At which time he patiently explained about the company's policy of shutting down all incoming and outgoing communications when a cruise ship signaled trouble using SSAS.

"That's bullshit," Charles proclaimed. "You had no warning until now. Is that right? You're the head of security," he poked McKenzie in the back with the gun.

John shrugged, and said, "Yes, on the ship. Not here.I don't have a clue about what the captain is talking about. That's above my pay grade."

Jeff added, "It told everybody you were taking over the ship a few minutes ago."

Charles actually looked shocked. His partner glared at him. For a moment, Jeff thought it would be Charles who would receive the bullet. Recovering, Charles said, "I don't want to go to San Diego, I have another destination in mind."

"Fine," Larson answered. "Be advised we only have enough fuel left for another three days, so it better not be timbuckfuckingtoo."

Jeff almost laughed out loud at Larson's use of the American vernacular and wondered where he had picked up the term. He decided that laughing out loud at this time might earn him a couple of bullets. He sensed Carmen begin to chuckle and gave her a light poke in the ribs to silence her. He said, "You and your buddies screwed the pooch, Charles. You should have come here first. Then you would have had it all. Your best bet is to lay low until San Diego and then exit with the crowd. Then you can get away and plan for another day. Hell, man, you've got the only photos we took. You're home free. Relax and enjoy the ship for a couple of days."

Charles walked around and looked at a dozen monitor screens, the two other officers giving way. All the screens were black.

"You mean we have no navigation?" Charles asserted.

Larson tapped a finger against his head.

"Shoot the first one that moves," Charles said to his partner. Tucking his gun in his rear waistband, he stepped back, pulled out his own phone, and punched in a single number. He tried it again. Then he tried several numbers. He got no connection.

"I told you," Larson said. "We're all in the same boat."

"We'll be back," Charles said. "You're coming with us," he told McKenzie.

At that, the three men departed the bridge. Larson asked one of his men to stand outside and let them know if anybody suspicious was approaching, then he turned to Wentworth and said, "All right, get powered up again, but leave off the WiFi. Get the hall cameras operational, specifically the director's office. They'll want to try the mike again."

Jeff added, "John won't be of use to them anymore. They'll probably lock him in the brig. With the captain's permission, I'd like to inform Butler of our situation. Wait a second, who's that?"

The camera picked up a third man who emerged from the director's office when Charles opened the door. His partner spoke with the third man who followed McKenzie to an elevator that went down to the same floor as the engines were located.

"That's where the brig is," Larson said.

Jeff said, "Mr. Wentworth, can you get a good close-up of that third man, along with anybody else that goes into the director's office? Your director is probably in the brig, too."

"Probably along with the watchman, who had the walkie talkie to alert SSAS in case of trouble. We are weaponized, you know," Larson noted.

"I'm sure you are. When do we need to turn on all systems," Jeff asked.

"We'll need to do that several hours out of San Diego," Larson answered.

"We may need to protect this bridge at that time. I think they're going to make one last ditch effort to get in here, even if it means shooting up the place," Jeff said. "

Larson nodded, and said, "Once we reach the point when we turn on all com systems, I'll have my people request that every passenger on top to go down below, then lock down both elevators to this level, as well as both stairways. I'll also post armed guards to prevent break-throughs, unobtrusive, of course.

Both men knew a shoot-em-up now would not do anyone any good. These were bad people who weren't afraid to die and take someone with them, a personality defect Jeff had been accused of having on more than one occasion.

Jeff rubbed his forehead, looked around him at the dark screens and said, "Somebody will definitely come back here periodically to ensure all our screen lights are still off. We need to contact Butler and your people, Sven."

Twenty nerve-wracking minutes later the systems were powered up, all calls had been made, and the photos sent to authorities in San Diego and elsewhere. As the evening wore on, Charles was seen to move casually about different levels of the ship making occasional contact with various men and women, pulling them aside and getting into heated discussions with them. Ortiz, who replaced Wentworth, worked his own shift and photographed them all.

Larson retired for the evening when the Staff Captain appeared at the door. The Staff Captain is second in command and in charge of navigation and the deck officers. A mate had been dispatched earlier to his cabin to inform him of developments.

Less than a single hour had passed since the announced takeover had begun. Time flies when you're having fun. With nothing else either of them could do, Jeff and Carmen left the bridge and decided to have dinner, as promised by their enemy. A movie tonight might be in the offing, unless Charles and his group came up with another plan. If they did, there would be no way to learn about it out until it was too late.

Half-way through the movie, Jeff realized he had out-thought himself. All of them were so caught up in their clever little plan—his clever little plan, actually—none of them thought to look ahead. Once they hit port, the ship would be in range of the towers there and the terrorists could send all the messages they wanted, all the while preventing the doors from opening.

"Let's go," he told Carmen in the middle of the movie.

"What now, Jeff?" she remarked. She was so tired of it all. After he quietly explained his concerns, she opted to remain to see the remainder of the movie.

During the next two days and nights, an armed man would appear at random times at the bridge, only to find the screens were still off.

Once the ship approached San Diego, Larson ordered all systems on. Armed with photographs of virtually every member of the errant group, arrests were made during disembarkation, including that of Charles. Following immediately behind him, Jeff spoke with authorities, who found and returned two phones belonging to him and Carmen.This was after personal verification from Larson and that of McKenzie, after considerable delay.

Few, if any, passengers were aware that anything out of the ordinary had occurred during the voyage, other than their inability to receive television programs, or to make electronic purchases. For this, the cruise line apologized profusely and offered discounts to anybody wishing to book another voyage with them.

To neutralize the terrorist threat, almost 1.5 million people in the city of San Diego had to go without cell phone service for several hours. Television reporters explained that faulty equipment made in China had caused the problem. From now on the providers promised to buy American. This scandal would never occur again. An investigation would take place, perhaps an international crisis might ensue.

Word had it that there was no shortage of hitmen going after Charles, while Jeff and Carmen disappeared like two water droplets in a fog bank. At their request, no mention of their role in the discovery and capture of the terrorists would occur.

Home at Last

When he returned from the lab, Jeff smelled carne asada and enchaladas warming on the stove top. He found Carmen seated in a lounge chair in their backyard. Pulling his chair closer to hers, he said, "Nice ring, there, Mrs. Shenero."

Carmen held it up to the last of the sunlight. "You think so?"

"I told you, I could have gotten you a bigger one," he said.

"And I told you it's not size that counts," she teased. "What matters is the loving intent."

"How does it feel to be invited to travel on a big cruise ship anywhere in the world anytime you want for the rest of your life for free?" Jeff asked.

"You tell me. Anyway, I don't know, yet. I'm still trying to get over the last vacation," Carmen replied, somewhat facetiously.

After a silence, with only the sound of cicadas in the trees, Jeff said, "Butler called me today at the lab after you left."

"And?"

"The man's name is Alexandr Vasiliev, a Russian, and he's not Marina's husband. The agency is thinking about hiring them both for purposes of counter-espionage, they're that good. You know, use them to track down other hackers. It's either hire take them in the fold or turn them over to Interpol where they'll spend the rest of their lives in prison."

"Like the counterfeiter who was so good they hired him to spot bad currency?" she asked.

Jeff nodded, "Exactly. Why waste the talent. Apparently, Jerry Richards was the brains behind the scheme. He got the relatives involved . . . although some wanted nothing to do with it . . . in order to raise money to pay for Marina and Vasiliev. Richards has a lot of relatives in jail now trying to post bond until their court date on a long list of charges. Each of them will have to repay what they received from their scheme, including having to sell their homes in some cases to pay back the cruise lines, who, by the way, have endless lawyers at their disposal."

Carmen chuckled and took a sip of wine. A glass of water stood in the second cup holder. "So the really bad international criminals who have stolen and continued to try and steal hundreds of millions get a cushy job with the feds in a gold mine and the little guy gets the shaft."

Jeff corrected her. "I wouldn't call fraud at the level this family was engaged in little guy games, especially considering their scheme to rip off the cruise line corporation. That particular line is owned by a country, not by individuals, so it's crimes against the state with a dozen felony charges against every one of them. No small potatoes."

Carmen said, "I guess the only positive thing going for Jerry is at least he stopped coughing."

After they stopped laughing, both were silent for some time. Carmen asked, "What are you going to do about the business, honey?"

"I don't know, I don't know," he mumbled, rubbing his hands over his face, very concerned.

A wash of guilt overcame Carmen. She had given him a hard time when she called him in India, to pull him home. She didn't trust his instincts when the poisonous products came to their house in her name and wouldn't speak to him for days about it. She badgered him into taking the cruise and had maneuvered him into marriage.

Now, here at home, supposedly safe and sound, he faced a conundrum, like a long string with the ends tied together and balled up. No matter where he began, he would go round and round to end up where he started from. He had disgruntled employees who had signed on for serious research on the verge of leaving, despite their high rate of pay. Less qualified people could do the same work his select staff were doing.

Jeff felt the same way they did, but he couldn't return the money. That's a no no. If he did, the word would be out and he could lose future grant monies. He might as well shut the doors. If he did accept grant money, he had to be careful not to co-mingle funds. Lawyers get disbarred for co-mingling. Scientists might face criminal charges, professors fired.

He needed to calm the troops, buy time, stay out of the limelight, and talk it over with some personal friends, but doing so went against one of his most basic tenets: Whatever you need to do, you can do it yourself. There had to be a solution.

Sharing these thoughts with his wife, she responded by contributing, "Honey, I know you never finished what you wanted to do in India. How about if we both go this time. You can explore all you want and I'll even go in the jungle with you, if it's all right. We'll take it easy and not get into any trouble. The employees can stand to be without you for another couple of weeks and it'll give you, us, a chance to concentrate on working out problems with your business from a distance without too many distractions. What do you say?"

Jeff took a deep breath and exhaled slowly and noisily. He looked directly into her dark eyes for a long time, then shook his head up and down. "You're right. We'll keep it nice and simple."

"Good. You can call it pleasure or you can call it business, but how are you going to explain to your employees you're going away again?" Carmen lamented.

Jeff replied, "I'll tell them we're leaving for personal reasons and when we come back we'll bring them good news."

Carmen raised her eyebrows and said, "You've

got me curious. Since you seem to have an answer for everything, what might that be?"

Jeff scratched his bald head and, with a sheepish look, said, "I wouldn't lie to you, dear. To tell the truth, I haven't got the slightest idea."

Return to India

After a light Chinese lunch on the wharf, Raj returned to make further arrangements for the evening's activities while Grace, Steven, and Henry took the couple to see the sights of the city, then returned them to their hotel to rest before the evening activities sponsored by the Rotary Club of Visak.

At 7:00 pm, Raj escorted them downstairs. Having been forewarned, and with great trepidation, Jeff and Carmen entered the meeting room to find it already packed with a portion of the front row reserved. The last two hours, they had spent time at the hotel's luxurious stores shopping for appropriate attire for the event.

Steven had contacted Raj to set up the gathering, after Jeff had announced that he would be coming. Everyone expressed enthusiastic joy in learning Carmen would be coming with him. No crazy train adventures to get there. This time the couple traveled first class all the way.

More than a hundred invited guests occupied the seats, many of whom belonged to Raj's immediate family. Others included dignitaries, movie stars, and many members of the upper crust of Indian society. Upon hearing the Sheneros would be coming to India, Raj, or rather his father, invited selected persons.

As current president of the club, Steven presented a lavish introduction of the couple, after which Jeff, thoroughly embarrassed, stood to begin the tale of his shipboard adventures. He omitted the story about the terrorists in Puerto Vallarta.

Most of the listeners were there to see him, but just as many were there to see Carmen, with her Bollywood looks. Many thought her dark complexion, large black eyes, black hair, trace of Aztecan nose, and enticing figure, would have looked better in a sari rather than in a skirt, or preferably, with nothing on at all, a sight reserved for Jeffrey Shenero alone, the bastard.

India had always been a marvelous blend of humanity, from the best to the worst, like any nation. But unlike any other nation, it possessed a multitude of languages, dialects, and religions, coupled with hard-core communists, terrorists, and fanatics, amidst a country filled with good folks. All were densely packed into a tight land mass with arguably the largest population density of any country on earth. Technology butted heads with ancient superstitions and the struggle to succeed butted heads with remnants of a caste system. Traveling across India was like traveling from New York to New Jersey, to Virginia and throughout the entire country. When a state line was crossed, the traveler would have to speak another language and learn another 56 or so letters of a new script. Yet, somehow, it worked.

Jeff had been to the country on other occasions, either for scientific conventions, or for purposes of exploration and had never encountered any serious personal threats. Now he had a wife in tow, one who announced the night before she wanted a child with him. He had problems with his own head, trying to convert living comfortably with someone he loved, into a life that put familial pressures on him, all of which challenged his sanity. Never mind terrorists. This had become serious. He told her they would talk about it more, once things calmed down and they could return to a stable life. Carmen did not seemed pleased with his answer.

Most of those present had either read or heard about the couple's ship adventure. If they hadn't, the Chatfields ensured they were teased with anecdotes about the second episode which never made the press, anecdotes the couple would share with them this evening.

After Steven made the introductions, Jeff began by presenting a quick review of events, beginning with his chance saving of the little girl to their meeting with LaMonde to relating what happened after the three criminals had been caught with their hands in the cookie jar.

Carmen stood by his side throughout, occasionally

filling in parts of the story.

They told the tale to an audience whose lives were enwrapped in soap operas, whether they were real life or on-screen. Steven had warned them that listeners expected to hear every little nuance so they could put themselves in his place. The more cringe-worthy they could make the story, the better.

At the end Jeff asked for questions.

Several hands were raised. He allowed Grace the honor of asking the first question. She sat next to Steven and Henry in the front row. "How did Richards know the top floor had its own air conditioning and why did he do it at all?"

Jeff said, "The first part was easy. The company advertised it in their literature in order to fill the expensive suites. Even if they hadn't, a man of Richards' skill could have easily found it out online, just like he found out the location of the A/C unit that served it by dredging up the blueprints for the vessel.

"The second part is something he's not talking about. We think it's because Carmen said she had a suite there and he strongly believed she wanted him to admit to a crime such as false claims about a disease. So he teased her with the truth without there being any evidence. By the time he got searched for the pepper, he had already loaded it onto the filter. To him, it seemed like a harmless prank. It wasn't like he added poison gas to the air. Unfortunately, that act alone added 20 years to his sentence. Richards was not a violent man, per se, but he did have a sense of vengeance. It's fair to say he's sworn off women since then. Actually, he has no choice."

The audience laughed again.

Jeff added, "In my experience, he could have done some serious damage if he had a mind to. I once encountered a similar circumstance where a terrorist added fungal toxin to an A/C unit in a sports arena. He also poisoned the filters on passenger planes. That memory gave me the idea of the air handlers being involved. Any other questions?"

One person asked, "If he thought Carmen was trying to trap him, why did Richards tell her about the plot to hack the cruise lines account?"

Jeff answered, "Great question. That never came up during the interrogation or in trial. The authorities were laser focused on gathering evidence for the crime itself to put these people away and to stop the ring. However, Carmen and I think that, despite his suspicions, he did feel her allure. Besides, he never told her the hackers were onboard, he only said he needed money for their hire sometime in the future. It became a he-said, she-said argument with no proof. Even if she reported what he said—which she did—he had a clean record and might simply be a person given to tell tales of fantasy. I think we have all met someone who can tell a good story with little truth to it.

"From what I'm told, he and Marina had been texting each other. He offered her the car, but she and Alexandr only dealt with cash, so he offered it to Carmen. Even after the job was completed, Jerry still needed to pay them the balance out of his portion of the theft, that's how hard core they were."

Jeff called on another person who said, "This question is for Carmen."

The man identified himself as a reporter for the *Times of India,* a world traveler himself, who asked, "Mrs. Shenero, what did you think when you and your husband got the same symptoms Richards had?"

She answered, "I thought: This is identical to the other symptoms even though I haven't been putting pepper up my nose. We began to wonder what made the upper level unique. Jeff put it all together."

Following their presentation, numerous guests crowded around Carmen for several minutes before the call came to begin the grand feast in the ballroom, a normal event for the hotel.

Jeff didn't see himself in the same light as others here saw him, detractors notwithstanding. He didn't bask in the light; in fact, he shunned it. He yearned to fully express himself verbally and professionally, yet withdraw into his turtle shell when it felt comfortable to do so. Unfortunately, fate dictated otherwise. He was destined to solve problems, many of which were of great magnitude. He sought not fame and glory, things just worked out that way. Honored at home, he found himself a celebrated guest in another country, while doing his best to wall it off.

Walking to the ballroom, Carmen at first refused lucrative movie offers from producers and wealthy businessmen who yearned to let her advertise for them. She replied she might do so, if proceeds would be channeled to charities of her choice.

At one point during the meal, Jeff leaned over to her said, "A word of advice. Watch out for the curry. It's crazy hot," to which Carmen replied, "I already had some. You call that hot? What a wimp."

While Jeff chatted, Carmen fell asleep in the backseat on the way to Raj's house on the outskirts of the city where they would remain for three days before moving in with the Chatfields, some 20 miles south in Bimli. The wayfarers would need a lot of sleep. Tomorrow, Raj and his driver would take them deep into the jungle of Srikukulam.

The Srikukulam Jungle

The Srikululam district of the state of Andhra Pradesh is renowned for its brassware products and cashews, along with a variety of other artistic goods. The pendulum swings the other way when one considers extremely primitive jungle dwellers who live among pythons and cobras. Jeff failed to mention these incidental factoids to Carmen, but ensured Raj carried a supply of anti-venin and other first-aid equipment. For himself, Jeff had his permits, instant ice-freeze packets, pocket microscope, an all-purpose utility tool on his belt, and a pistol loaded with buckshot rounds Raj had given both him and Carmen.

Entering the dense thicket of the jungle covering the northern coast of the state, the Jeep's driver carefully negotiated a small rutted road leading them beneath the canopy and out of the sunlight. Occasionally Raj would make a comment such as. "Watch out or snakes crossing the road," or "Last month a sloth bear walked through one of the villages we're going to visit," or "I hope you put on plenty of insect repellent."

Finally, Carmen laughed. "If you're trying to test me, Raj, don't try. My father used to take me to visit old archaeological sites buried deep in the jungles of Mexico, especially the one near where we lived in Guadalahara."

Jeff sat up straight and said, "You never told me did archaeological exploration."

Carmen replied, simply, "Honey, you never asked," which caused Raj laughed in turn.

At one point, as the Jeep approached a small stream, Jeff said, "Hold on. This area looks ripe for picking." The driver stopped the vehicle and Jeff got out to look more closely at the various life forms growing on softened woody debris in the slow moving water. "We'll stop here in the way back," he announced.

Raj said, "We crossed a lot of streams, Jeff, how are you going to know this one?"

Jeff held up a finger in the universal language meaning "Wait a minute," and from his backpack pulled out a roll of yellow tape. He began to string it from one tree to another. The tape read in black lettering: CRIME SCENE—POLICE LINES—DO NOT CROSS. On second thought, he re-rolled the tape, then took several minutes to carefully collect his samples while the others watched his exactitude. "Better to get them while I'm here in case it's dark when we get back," he announced.

Once underway again, Jeff asked Raj, "Is this first village the one you told us about yesterday where everybody has the skin disease?"

"Yes, the same one," Raj replied.

"Did you manage to find the chemicals we requested?" Carmen asked.

"Yes, the container is either in the back or on the roof with the other supplies," Raj said.

The village appeared to be comprised of some 40-50 huts. As they approached, the driver blew the horn several times to inform those working in the nearby rice paddies of their arrival. Several of the men began to unload specified items from the car, including a side of pork Raj had obtained from somewhere. Although many of the natives held religious beliefs against eating meat or even pork, survival reigned as the god almighty and trumped other beliefs which could be temporarily discarded.

On the outskirts of the collection of huts, Jeff noted a light pole with a shaded light and power wires he hadn't seen on their drive. The country was making a great effort to electrify outlying villages. Whether the lights came on or not might be a different story, thanks to power shortages, especially during storms and overuse of fans and A/C units during the hot season.

From what the visitors could see, these people weren't exactly making bronze statuettes to sell to tourists. The place resembled an outpost. Most villages in the country had light switches on the walls and a good percentage of the public at large had television. This place had snakes, bears, and three-inch very nasty red scorpions, along with mold reportedly growing on their skin.

Women arriving from the paddies had their saris hiked up to expose their upper thighs. One of them approached this strange woman who had just arrived who wore a baseball cap, tan work shirt, blue jeans, and work boots Raj had scrounged up from somewhere. She handed Carmen her lit cigar from her own mouth. Carmen graciously put it in her mouth, took a drag, coughed, and handed it back, to the great amusement of the others. She had been initiated. Jeff thought about telling them his wife was a movie star, but doubted if any of them had ever been to the cinema. Besides, their idea of personal hygiene differed from that of regular movie goers and in all likelihood, they wouldn't have been admitted into the theater.

Jeff quickly identified the fungal disease afflicting the natives as Tinea Versicolor, a yeast infection demarked by discolored patches of the skin. The patches had sharp margins and caused occasional itching due to continually moist skin providing an environment suitable for the yeast to grow.

With Carmen treating the women in one hut and Jeff treating the men in another, they applied a solution of copper sulfate with cotton balls onto the various areas. Raj told the natives to expect another application in the evening, which should finish the treatment, although it could take weeks for the skin to return to its normal appearance.

In addition to the meat, the chief presently had in his possession several one-pound cans of ground coffee, iodine, bandages, and two large jugs of whiskey. There would be a feast tonight, something these people seemed to relish like a dog gobbling up good food before other dogs could get to it. Tomorrow would take care of itself.

While dropping off supplies to two other villages, Jeff had collected a number of other mold samples, while Carmen had sutured a gashed leg, shot a cobra that had slithered into one of the huts, and delivered twins.

When they returned, darkness had fallen. The single electric light on the pole cast eerie stretched-out shadows over the compound. With the fire blazing, the party goers feasted and sang among the beasts and insects of the jungle, as their ancestors had done many years in the past. It wasn't Amazonia, but you'd never know the difference. Jeff loved this simple life in the land time forgot, at least for a one night stand. Gatherings such as these highlighted the superficialities brought about by wealth and always gave him cause to appreciate the basic goodness of human nature when people were free from governmental overreach without reliance on material goods.

The Indus Valley was one of the three oldest civilizations on the planet, along with Egypt and Mesopotamia. Evidence pointed to its settlement during the Bronze Age, some 5000 years in the past and some 3000 years before the Chinese established their strongholds. Humans migrated downward into the sub-continent and many found their way to this locale, with the Bay of Bengal only two miles to the east, subject to occasional typhoons. Except for the clothing, the drums and dancing might be similar to that of their ancestors. In one sense, he felt comfort in knowing some things never change.

To the chief's great delight, Jeff awarded him the roll of colorful police tape for his personal usage. What he might do with the gift was irrelevant.

Once home, Raj offered to put Jeff's samples on dry ice and have his people airfreight them back to Jeff's lab. The couple spent the next several days as guests of Raj and his immediate family. Saying their goodbyes three days later, they moved in with the Chatfields, where they relaxed, read, and walked on the beach at night, where no city lights could wash out the stars of the galaxy shown edge-on.

On their second day, Jeff could contain himself no longer. After dinner, and in the presence of Henry and Steven——Grace collared Carmen to give her a tour of her shell collection——Jeff opened up about his logistics problem at work and with the government. Henry suggested, "Why don't you build an add-on to your own facility and hire who you need? This will allow you and your people to get back to doing the research you love."

Steven offered, "Or, you can sub out the work to one of our numerous affiliates. The closest one to you would be in Kansas City, Missouri. It's close enough for you to keep a watchful eye on it from your place in Oklahoma. Since you're under the aegis of the Consumer Product Safety Commission, the head of whom I helped get appointed, you should get approval for the shift and not have to spend time constructing an add-on. The FDA won't be involved because we're not dealing with food or drugs.

"I should think the approval and the shift could take place within three months, maybe two. It shouldn't be complicated. It might seem new to you, but these things go on all the time."

The next day would see their departure, not for home, but to begin an episode in Carmen's life which should go smoothly. But with Jeff around, one could never know what dangers might circle them in dark waters. If some people found themselves in harm's way, Jeff would find his way into harm's maw.

Overkill

During the great banquet following their presentation in Visak, Carmen had made a commitment to do magazine cover shoots. Steven had advised her to expect a few complications. Photography wasn't his area of expertise, but legal pitfalls were. He set her up with a law firm accustomed to working with movie stars and other personages in exactly this manner, protecting their integrity and ensuring they received the best money possible. In her case, the money would go to her designated charities.

One thing she could be certain of, whatever made the press in India would make the press in the States simply because the rights to pictures can be sold or transferred to sister periodicals owned by the same corporations. These sister periodicals also had affiliates in Europe and Asia. Agreeing to this would bring everyone more money, including the orphanages.

"Do we want to do this, Jeff?" Carmen asked. She had dredged up the same sense of reluctance that had overcome her aboard ship heading for an unwanted meeting with Richards. Except that now she had become the fish to be caught and she knew the identity of the sharks chasing her, perhaps with other swimmers lurking nearby waiting to feast on any remains.

Once known as Bombay, Mumbai is India's largest city with a population of some 22 million in its greater metropolitan area. It is the country's financial center and the heart of the Bollywood film industry, arguably the largest producer of movies of any country in the world. In addition, newly minted Vogue and GQ were headquartered there. They became so popular a read that a full one-third of their monthlies were filled with advertisements.

Because the cover of Vogue displayed both sexes, the magazine became interested in the married couple, each worthy of display. GQ expressed more interested in Jeff than Carmen, having retrieved from somewhere an earlier picture of him in Speedos, shirtless, and cut like a gymnast. Between his shaved head, oriental eyes and prominent scar, not to mention his overall square fame, he became ripe fodder. The legal firm engaged by Steven put their staff to work on it. Money was no problem for anyone, but a loss of personal integrity could make it all meaningless for the couple, if a single misstep should occur.

"Honey, we can always back out," Jeff offered.

"Children's charities will always exist, with or without us. We can up the donations we already make without having to do this."

Despite her expressed reluctance to go through with upcoming events, once again, Carmen felt a certain thrill of diving into danger. She wasn't so naïve as to ask herself "What could go wrong?" Simply believing that to be a valid question could be a forerunner to lengthy hate-yourself episodes. These would be similar to those that ravaged her when she had a chance to finish her medical degree, but chose to stick with Jeff, instead. All right, it worked out for the best. She chose a good path, but it took a long time for the regrets to go away. Unfortunately, all the regrets were resurfacing.

If she were to believe her superstitious husband, one should not believe the words: "See, you expected bad things to happen, but everything turned out all right." To him, having no expectations cleared the mind and minimized the chance of failure. When you think about protesting before the challenge, you lose the gold medal. Get the gold medal first, then file your complaint.

Vogue insisted they be picked up by helicopter on the first morning for reasons of publicity, wanting the media to film the new celebrities arriving on the rooftop of the building. It didn't matter they could walk there from their hotel.

At 6:45 am, the couple sat in the hotel lobby, waiting. At 7:00 am sharp, a low noise became louder as helicopter landed in the courtyard, causing the building to shake and window to vibrate. Guests rushed to look out, thinking the world might be coming to an end.

Jeff smiled sheepishly at the hotel clerk. "That's for us," he said. A man came out a side door of the machine to lead them to the aircraft. Holding her hand, Jeff led her to the noisy machine, not often seen on the hotel grounds, while Carmen hunkered down to protect her hair from the whirlwind. The man opened a side door for them and helped them enter, take their seats, buckle in, and gave them noise-cancellation headsets to communicate with the pilot. Then he climbed into the passenger side next to the pilot.

The pilot tested the headsets and Jeff acknowledged by replying, "There's some place I'd like to go to first, if you can."

"Sir, I'll have to call it in for permission," replied the pilot. "Where is it you want to go?"

Jeff told him. The pilot received the okay and a moment later, he lifted off, headed straight west about 100 yards then made a sharp turn northward up the coast only a few miles. Shortly, the airship flew slowly over the largest ship graveyard in the world. Scores of ships lined the beachfronts two and three deep with piles of metal on the beach reminding Jeff of pictures he had seen of remote islands that displayed millions of tons of plastics washed up on their shores. But here everything was compartmentalized: furniture, glass, larger pieces of metal, machinery, smaller metal objects as far as the eye could see with thousands of workers weaving in and out of the scrap, cutting, torching, and carrying pieces to waiting trucks. No derricks and cranes here, as in Turkey and elsewhere. The gravity method on these shores meant that heavier objects were usually hand or machine pushed off upper decks into the already highly contaminated water. The big money came from the recycled steel, not from the dead fish that could be found miles out to sea.

"Down there is where I grew up, sir," said the pilot.

"How's so?" Carmen asked, flabbergasted at the sight, starring out the window, fixated on the thousands of human-like ants crawling over and around pieces of metal or climbing onto higher structures of the ships.

"I worked there every day for three years, seven days a weeks in my early teens," replied the pilot. "Summer, winter, monsoons, it didn't matter. "He held up his right arm where an angry burn mark remained. "Backed into a red hot piece of metal for part of my pay."

"Did you get medical?" Carmen asked, without thinking.

"Sure did. Wrapped it up and went back to work the next day," laughed the pilot. "Went back to my five brothers and sisters and tried to study. Kept seeing these planes flying overhead and wanted to be like them some day."

"And here you are," said Jeff.

"Yes, sir," agreed the pilot.

Reaching the end of the graveyard, the pilot was about to bank left for the turn-around when Jeff said, "Wait, what's up ahead?"

"It's the city dump," answered the copilot.

"It's huge," Jeff remarked.

"Yes, sir," the man agreed. "The mountain of trash in the middle is a good 120 feet tall. You're looking at some 300 acres of city garbage collected over a hundred years."

Flying over the dump, again human worker-ants could be seen crawling over the countless items, picking scraps where they could for personal use or for sale. The co-pilot contributed, "You people have landfills. This is how we dispose of our waste. There are some 3000 places like these in our country, some large, some small. Although, there is talk about building a recycling plant here."

"How would that work?" Jeff inquired. "You'd have to hand-separate out the plastics and the smaller metal objects. You've got to have lead and cadmium in there. You couldn't burn those elements or the plastic unless you wanted to kill off half the population."

"Sorry," concluded the pilot, in a tone suggesting he didn't want to think about the problem. "Not our area of expertise."

An instant later, he said, "Hang on, we're going back." He banked hard left and returned past the ship graveyard, this time a little farther out to sea.

The copilot picked up the story. "I used to fly freight in the Middle East. You get out to Turkey and you might see a number of modern cruise ships getting trashed, big ones, too. Some 800 ships a year get decommissioned. Companies lost billions during COVID with nobody wanting to sail anymore. Ships got sold at auction to end up at unregulated places like this for twice the money and sold for millions in scrap. Figure it takes at least a year to dismantle each ship. Steel is worth a lot. Here in India, asbestos isn't considered hazardous, neither is lead. It's recycled into building materials."

"Beauty and the beast," Carmen laughed, not out of humor, but out of irony. "We recently sailed on one of those monsters. Is there nothing permanent anymore?"

"How sad," Jeff lamented. He felt as she did, recently having been integrated with a living breathing sea-going giant creature that, at any moment, could be stripped down to its bones on dead shores somewhere. He tried to put a finger on his feelings. Perhaps it was the ignoble end to man's genius that disturbed him so much, from the countless billions of tons of plastics created to make life easier that floated or sank in the seas of the world or washed up onto shores, to the broken ships that began to serve his pleasures, to the throw-away trash in general, never mind what couldn't be seen.

No, more than that, nothing could or would be done about it. Perhaps one day the Earth itself might shake off the surface detritus like a dog shaking-off, in an effort to get itself reorganized.

"Prepare for landing," declared the pilot. The

visitors looked out to see the helicopter approach a large X on the roof the Vogue/GQ building after only 20 minutes off schedule. Numerous reporters and cameras of every ilk awaited them.

The Vogue building was located on the first floor of a large complex of buildings in the financial district of Mumbai, with Gentlemen's Quarterly occupying the second floor of the Conde Nast Indian magazine empire, situated only a mile to the north of the famous Taj Majal Palace Hotel. Reportedly, the hotel had the reputation of having been built backwards with the arms of the U-shaped structure and the inner courtyard reaching out toward a back alley, rather than toward the bay itself. Because of this, many superstitious Indians believed the hotel brought bad luck and shied away from booking a room there—the same hotel where the Sheneros were staying.

The first day at Vogue, a Friday, began with the signing of documents which had to do with rights and privileges and financial considerations, all of which had been prearranged. Following legal proceedings, Jeff was introduced to a middle-aged extremely handsome Indian who had retired from the movie business to take up an executive position with the magazine, while a guide introduced Carmen to his female counterpart.

A tour of the facilities followed the legal aspects to include their respective make-up rooms, editorial areas, photography, break room, and managerial offices. The actual printing occurred at another location which received copy via electronic transmission to create the slick magazines bringing in many millions of dollars annually.

By 6:00 pm, the couple left the building. Their driver awaited them at the door with the car parked just outside. A large crowd was forming to begin the celebration of a holiday and the driver aggressively pushed people aside in order to open the back door of the car. "It's Diwali," he announced.

The festival of lights, Jeff had read, was the biggest celebration of the year celebrated by Hindus, Sikhs and Jains, with gift giving, the lighting of candles, and displays of fireworks. The event celebrated light over darkness, good over evil, spiritual awakening, human betterment over bad intent, five days that interrupted businesses accustomed to such interruptions.

The next day, Saturday, work began at 7:00 am with an hour of make-up for Jeff and over three hours for Carmen. They went through various poses and clothing changes. Jeff had an early panic attack, slamming himself for getting involved in this business in the first place. He had no problem with those who accidentally fell into an opportunity and took advantage of it. However, he openly loathed those who took advantage of their celebrity to flaunt themselves simply for financial gain.

Yet, here he was doing exactly the same thing, wasn't he? He had to tell himself, *No, Jeff. You're doing this because you want to give it all to children's orphanages here in India and back home, to find better foster parents for them, to get them good medical attention. And you'll do whatever it takes to make that happen.* Once he reminded himself of his purpose, the problem went away.

The workday finished at 8:00 pm. The driver nervously awaited inside the front door along with a security guard. Outside, a slowly moving current of people flowed from south to north, jammed more tightly than the laws of physics should allow. The guard unlocked the door to the building, the trio exited, and the guard locked the door behind them to disappear into the building to make his rounds. Holding Carmen's hand, Jeff took a few steps to the curb where the sedan stood, the river of humans flowing around it like it were flotsam in a stream. The driver tried to open the door, but got swept away in the current followed by Carmen and then Jeff.

Jeff tried to see her black hair among a populace of a billion black-haired people, all of whom appeared at this one location, to be moving together, cheering, waving lighted signs, dressed in every color imaginable.

It reminded him of the time he went to the Oklahoma-Texas football game down in Dallas back in the old days, when the river flowed in one direction, making a long circuit as directed by law enforcement, occasionally passing a liquor store. He would purchase a six-pack at three times the going rate, and drink it along the circuit until the next pass. Was this flow going in a circuit?

His hotel was a mile back in the other direction

and he had lost his wife. Although she had her cell in her clutch, he had left his back in the hotel on purpose. Why would one want to bring a phone to a photo shoot? He was proud of himself for manning up by leaving it behind without having the feeling of nakedness one normally feels when it is accidentally left behind. He wouldn't need to make calls or take pictures. At the moment, however, he believed he might have been in error.

For Carmen's part, she started out the day tired. Now she was tired and hungry. Except for a brief respite for lunch in the building cafeteria, she'd been on her feet all day. She was so looking forward to a Kobe steak and a relaxing drink of tea, comparing notes with her husband, laughing about the various poses they had to go through.

Pushed by the mass of humanity, her life seemed to her to be no different than a single bird in a great murmur, swaying to and fro, pushing forward, until it hit a log jam, which would soon break free, only to surge forward again, with no particular destination in mind. Countless people carried lighted pole flags and banners waving like wheat in a breeze. Nowhere could she see vehicular traffic of any kind. She thought about working her way to the edge and finding a store to shelter in, but everything was closed. Why didn't anybody tell them about this holiday? Would this be an all-nighter?

She had grown up with large celebrations in Mexico, such Dia de los Muertos, and had been to Mardi Gras with Jeff, but this was other worldly, appearing like a happy riot, no government to overthrow, no economic protests, just a lot of people celebrating.

Wait, she could still make a call. But to whom? 911? She tried to forget about her problems when she realized her husband probably had the same issues, trying to get to their hotel, any hotel, all behind them. Suddenly, firecrackers went off, causing the great beast to pulsate. She made an effort to get to the very edge of the crowd so she would not be completely surrounded, thus minimizing the chances of being crushed.

After what seemed like an hour to Carmen, who was being buffeted like a ping pong ball in a closed space, the saw the road split into three. Hugging the near edge of the crowd, she flowed with it along the left branch and within a short time, saw a large bearded policeman armed with a baton, but no firearm. He did not encourage loitering in the thinning crowd, but probably wouldn't mind five twenty dollar bills in his pocket. She had long since discarded her small clutch, placing her cell in her pocket along with her hotel key card. She needed both hands for this fight.

Approaching the policeman, she put both palms together in a *namasthe* gesture and asked, "Can you help me?"

She did not know Marathi, the language of the state of Maharastra; however, she had learned a few words of Hindi, not exactly the defacto official language of the country, but close enough. For

God's sake, this was still the financial district of the country, the man might even speak English.

The policemen took in this disheveled creature who, clearly, did not belong to the crowd, and replied, in a sing song rhythm, "Just I am helping you."

The man spoke English. Carmen said, simply, "I am American. I am lost. I am staying at the Taj Mahal Royal Hotel. Can you find me a ride there? I will pay." She pulled out the money she had folded into a small rectangle and handed it to the man. He took it, looked at it, smiled, and said, "Come."

She followed him around a corner onto a dark lonely street, concerned she might have gone from the frying pan into the fire. She had the sudden urge to run, back into the crowd, if necessary, mentally reviewing the self-defense moves Jeff had taught her, until she saw the man lead her toward a small scooter chained to a tree. He unlocked it, tucked the chain into a small box on the rear, and patted the tiny seat behind his own.

Carmen took the seat, precariously balancing on the end, and found a set of foot pegs, while her personal driver sped through the back streets of Mumbai. Carmen wrapped her arms tightly around the big man in front of her, keeping her head down. Heavy traffic flowed along the side streets, the main thoroughfare blocked by revelers. For an instant she had a humorous thought: *Who's going to try and stop a scooter driven by a policeman weaving in and out of traffic with a woman on the back? There's something to be said for alternative lifestyles.*

In the major and minor cities, of the country, literally hundreds of thousands slept on sidewalks and in the street itself, near their small stall or store. Not so in this section of Mumbai with its glitter of glass and tall buildings, with no small stalls to be found.

Only short minutes later, they reached the front of the brightly lit hotel. Carmen dismounted, kissed her savior on the cheek and said, "Thank you," once again. *Let him tell that story back at the police station,* she thought, smiling at the broad grin on the man's face. She wondered what the final version would be.

Carmen took the elevator to their suite and called the dining room to place her order. After a cool shower, a little hair brushing and a change of clothes, she prepared to go downstairs to eat, thinking, *Jeff can take care of himself. I'll bet he's probably trapped somewhere with no way out, just the way he likes it.*

Nothing so complicated. A quarter hour behind Carmen, Jeff found the same side street she had, but at least he didn't have to worry about rapists or thieves, especially if he ran.

Time is relative depending on perception. An hour in a crowd moving at half-a mile per hour can seem like a ten-mile-long trek. He began an easy jog, reading a brightly lit billboard promoting birth control: LOOP BEFORE YOU LEAP.

Just as Carmen closed her room door to go down

to dinner, Jeff appeared. "What a coincidence," he declared, sweat running from every pore. "You never know who you'll run into when you travel. Don't you look nice and refreshed? Did you have a good time?"

Overjoyed to see him safe, Carmen had learned to joke about a bad situation. "There's no justice. I can't even run away from my husband." She gave him a quick kiss on the lips, the second man she'd kissed in the past half-hour. "I'll go down and order for you," she concluded.

Jeff took a cold shower, changed, and met his wife downstairs for a satisfying dinner and conversations about their day's adventures. Tomorrow would be an off-day, with more make up sessions and poses looming ahead early next week. Tonight and tomorrow belonged to them.

The Agent Orange Epidemic

One

Flies are attracted to raw meat. The Sheneros fit into this category. A month after returning home from India, a magazine representative called to inform them that the next American and British additions of Vogue and GQ would soon run stories about them coupled with different photos than those used in India. This information mildly upset the pair, who had promised each other to seek obscurity forevermore.

On the following day, Jeff received a video call on his private computer office/lab line. The image of Emily Kaufman appeared on screen. He philosophically labeled such occurrences "collision of converging waves resulting from major events."

"Good morning, Emily," he said cheerily. "Do you have another discovery so soon on the heels of the last one?"

Emily didn't laugh. "Yes, doctor" —— she insisted on using formalities rather than calling him by his first name —— "but it's more an observation rather than a discovery. You know how *Jeffrus shenerii* needs oil to produce spores and to proliferate? Well, there are oils and there are oils."

"Let me pass your knowledge along to the staff," Jeff said, in his most sarcastic manner. Emily knew he was teasing her in his patented manner to get her to speak her mind and meant no harm by the statement.

"It grows on anything with oil," she threw out, teasing back, testing him.

"Like bacon or salad dressing or motor oil?" Jeff guessed.

"Yes, and like human skin, doctor. We have a small epidemic here in the building," she threw out.

"You mean everybody is turning orange?" Jeff laughed.

"Yes."

"Shit."

"That's what Arnold said. I'm sending you some pictures."

Jeff turned to his computer and opened her email message, then made a quick call to Carmen to join him. He split the screen with Emily's picture on one half and the pictures she sent on the other half. A chill ran up his spine, as though he was staring at photos of bears standing on their heads with the caption: *What's Wrong with this Picture?*

Arms and heads of men and women were

depicted. Each had orange to orange-red splotches tending to run together with normal appearing skin between them. He could see Emily patiently watching him examine the picture when Carmen came in. He motioned for her to take a seat, quickly summarizing the circumstances. Her eyes widened when he did so.

Leaning into the computer for a closer look she said, "Emily, what if this gets loose into the public at large?"

"I don't want to think about it," Emily admitted, with a sense of dread in her voice.

Two

Each mold has its preferences. The black mold *Stachybotrys* is most happy when it can grow on high carbon low nitrogen substances such as drywall or glue-down mastic; *Cladosporium* loves not only leaves, but paint and rubber; the ringworm fungi like the keratin in the skin and nails; and this new mold, buried in permafrost, prefers oil.

Jeff summarized, "It wouldn't produce spores on the tar paper when I first found it, but once it got fed short chain hydrocarbons, it became infectious."

"Correct," Emily replied. "It can be transferred from person to person, but it may also become infectious via airborne spores. We don't know. It could be either or both."

"What are you doing to contain it?" he inquired, in a *déjà vu* moment returning him to a conversation he'd had not long before onboard ship.

"Everything we can," Emily replied. "Each microbiological lab here has independent surgical room filtration, so there's no air mixing from one to another, but still we have people getting the infection who are not even associated with the labs. Maybe it gets transferred from person to person in the break room. We're limiting its growth by wiping ourselves down with rubbing alcohol to remove the surface oils, but we can't do it forever. I'm sending you another group of pictures. These represent the 'after'. You just looked at the 'before'."

She continued, "So far, only six of us have it, including Arnold and me. Nobody's going anywhere."

More photos appeared on-screen with the same arms and heads, but only an orange cast could be noted. Emily gave the couple time to examine the new group of pictures, then said, "We think the spores are still embedded, but it's way too early to know much more. Arnold wanted me to bring you into the loop, doctor. Six or eight of us are working on this, but we need all the help we can get."

Jeff actually laughed, his trademark response to pressure. He announced, "Glad you called, since the damn thing is named after me."

"Have you checked your animal facilities?" Carmen asked.

Emily answered, "Yes, and we're not seeing anything beneath the fur. They, too, are on an independent air purifying system. We check every day."

Carmen said, "As I recall, sebaceous glands are most numerous on the face and scalp, especially the nose. Human sebum is a mixture of triglycerides, fatty acids, waxes, and cholesterol. Our friend has plenty to choose from."

"Which is no help at all except to give us more avenues to explore," Emily summarized. "Arnold's supervisor is real close to calling the CDC, but he wanted me to call you first. I'm worried, Jeff," Emily said, in a rare use of his first name.

Emily began punching the keyboard. In an instant, new images appeared. The couple stared at the screen with heads almost touching as they looked at pictures of threads interwoven among square-off bodies. Neither said a word. The photos depicted skin scrapings of threads of mycelium in and around cuboidal skin cells about 10 times larger than they were. Mold spores were giving rise to germ tubes like Bermuda grass seeds sprouting and spreading runners both beneath and on top of the earth. Except the threads in the pictures were also penetrating the cell membranes of the skin cells.

"Phospholipids and sterols," Carmen said, referring to the composition of cell membranes. She didn't need to elaborate. In addition to using the sebum, the mold sought the lipid components of membranes to feed itself.

After a moment, Emily said, "Symptoms are insane itching, which, of course, will drive the spores and mycelium in deeper when scratched. This is coupled with paranoia, because nobody knows what the outcome will be. You're looking at my arm. The alcohol temporarily eases the itching, but it's way too early to see if there are any systemic reactions.

"Every exposed person gets a daily blood test. Arnold's super wants to shift another dozen people onto the project, but nobody wants the assignment unless we go to Bio-Containment Level 4, which is what we're doing. Things are moving pretty fast around here."

Emily could be seen trying to gather herself, look off to nowhere, and return to the screen, but seemed to be at a loss of words. Tears came to her eyes and she shook her head back and forth a couple of times, obviously loathe to what she had to say until she said it, "We're in big trouble."

To Jeff, the word "we" has a lot of implications. He said, "It's not my decision to make, obviously, but I'd leave the CDC out of it. First, it's an in-house lab occurrence—you can't even call it an accident. It doesn't affect the public at large. The last thing you need is for the feds to stick their noses into it."

A noise could be heard behind Emily. She turned to see Arnold take a seat next to her. The presence of orange tinges on his nose, temples, cheeks, and forehead confirmed the previously infected areas.

"Arnold, how nice to see you," Jeff quipped.

"Very funny," Arnold had to laugh, knowing what he looked like. "A small bit of information: The wife of one of our infected men just called to say their two children have the disease. In a word, it got loose."

"There's a Mongolian Cluster Fuck, if I ever saw one," Jeff said, fully aware that any hackers tuning in on this conversation, who claimed Mongolian ancestry, might take offense at the racist statement and report him for hate crimes against humanity.

He said, "You have no choice but to call the feds. Over at Chatfield, you people are better equipped to investigate this problem than I am, but if you'll tell me what you've found out so far and send me your new data, I'll do what I can to help from here. Everyone is going to have to work fast because it appears this new contagion waits for no one."

Three

Ringworm is a term reserved for three genera of soil fungi that attack the keratin in hair, skin, and nails of humans and other mammals. The disease forms ring-like patterns as the mold grows outward from a central point. It can be transferred from one person to another via contact, or from one part of the body to another when scratching is involved.

Jeff contemplated this strangely colored skin-related mold that grew in patches, not in ring-like patterns—more like the skin yeast he found attacking the tribe in India. He felt sorry for his friends in Boston who couldn't devote the time required to continue their investigations into the positive aspects of the mold. Instead, they had become consumed with trying to keep it from attacking them, like a dog snapping at a kind master.

Both Jeff and Carmen knew what the feds would

do. They had no option. They would quarantine the residences of the three men and one woman who were infected, and quarantine the Kaufman home. And rightly so. A hazmat team would post a big radioactive sign on the door with yellow tape and QUARANTINED — DO NOT ENTER signs all over the place. Their families would be trapped for an indefinite period of time. Their neighbors would go ballistic, the press would go nuclear.

Furthermore, the six affected employees of the company would remain in isolation, not permitted to leave the building. Cots would have to be brought up to them for sleeping along with their meals, and their activities would be limited. A warm touchy-feely research expedition just became a nightmare, and not reporting its presence would be unthinkable. This thing could spread faster than a California wildfire, unless it got contained immediately. Fortunately, although several scientists at big pharma were infected, they still had access to top-of-the-line research equipment, but lacked direction.

As off-putting as these events might seem, the picture became more complex. The infected housewife had left work early to visit her hair salon and then visited the supermarket before going home to celebrate her son's birthday with friends; one of the three men had gone to his usual bar after work; another had stopped at a hardware store; and the third man had waited in a line to fill a prescription.

When the press in Boston ran the story of the outbreak, a full 50 people claimed to be infected with demonstrable rashes and another 150 who only made the claims. An astute reporter covering the science beat saw Jeff's name out of the information dump, a name shining like a spotlight in a dark room. *Jeffrus Shenerii,* sounded an awful lot like Jeffrey Shenero.

Four

AP

The CDC announced the presence of a new skin infection. It appears to have its origin in the Boston area. Authorities believe it may have escaped from a laboratory where experimental work was being conducted with the agent, but denounces its similarity to the COVID-19 virus that escaped the Wuhan, China, laboratory. Any mention of a pandemic caused by this new disease is unwarranted.

According to experts, scientist Jeffrey Shenero first discovered the agent while visiting India and brought it back to Boston for further study at Chatfield laboratories, well-known for the manufacture of numerous widely used pharmaceuticals.

Mr. Shenero, who owns and operates his own research facility in Norman, Oklahoma, is widely known for his unraveling of various criminal plots. Sources say he is assisting Chatfield Pharmaceuticals with their efforts to find a cure for the orange-colored disease. He says it is similar to ringworm, a world-wide skin infection caused by mold. Both can present extreme itching and discomfort on the parts of the body with the most oil glands—the outline of a face and body appeared with arrows pointing to the primary areas of infection. *Both are spread by contact, but the new disease, dubbed Agent Orange——a throwback to a toxic chemical used during the Vietnam era——seems appropriate.*

Mr. Shenero says there are major differences between the two types of infective agents. While ringworm fungi will grow in constantly moist areas of the body, Agent Orange can grow anywhere on the body at any time, except for the soles of the feet and palms, although it prefers more oily areas such as the face and scalp where triglycerides, oils, sugars, and waxes are naturally produced to protect the body against evaporation.

Unlike ringworm, many confirmed cases of the new disease appear to cure spontaneously. Investigators are at a loss as to the cause of this.

Like Jeff, the first thought of conspiracy theorists would point to the government's denial of Agent Orange's similarity to COVID-19s escape from Wuhan, which absolutely proved the two were identical in that manner. Therefore, the government is lying. What else is new?

Jeff stayed up late pouring over the data initially submitted by Emily and Arnold when she first contacted him aboard ship. He hand-plotted sets of numbers on a simple x and y axis, numbers appearing to be random at first, and saw a downward slope. The growth rate of the mold decreased when the pH increased. It refused to grow at an alkaline pH above

8.0. He looked up the pH of human sebum, the term used for human skin oil, and found it to be 5.6-5.8. Could the solution to the problem be as simple as this?

The next morning he called Boston with Carmen seated next to him. Emily appeared on-screen. When Jeff explained what he had in mind, Arnold's orange face appeared. "That's crazy, man." he said.

"I told him that too," Carmen added.

"Let's find out," Emily said, and broke the connection.

AP

The Shenero Institute for Medical Research, Chatfield Laboratories, and the CDC is recommending the following for elimination of the new disease-causing agent dubbed Agent Orange:

Wash your face and body with bar soap (pH of 9-10)

For those interested in more traditional treatments, a list of medications and treatments is listed below:

Jeff rubbed his forehead, wishing he could live in a remote village somewhere, herding goats, fishing, or planting rice, anything but this. He wasn't meant to live in a civilized nation during modern times. If he could go back to, say, 20,000 B.C., he would only need a sturdy club to conk things with and a good woman. Maybe he could start a brewery. That way everybody would protect him and love him at the same time.

His cell phone dinged with an incoming message. *What now?* he thought, looking at the screen to read.

Jeff, old boy: I see you made the news again. Thank you for helping us come out on top. Your instant cure saved us from having to chase our tails forever and spending a fortune. With the CDC on your side, the quarantines were lifted and my people were able to get back to their normal lives. As always, stop by when you're in the neighborhood. P.S. Grace has your picture from the cover of GQ Magazine posted on her wall. I'm not sure I'm too happy about it. In retaliation, I posted a picture of Carmen from Vogue. Regards from Henry.

Steven Chatfield

P.S. Thank you for accepting my offer to shift your project to Kansas City. My man in Washington tells me he'll take care of the paperwork.

Long months of worry had come to an end with this missive from Steven. He could finally call a general staff meeting to inform the troops about the good news he had on hold. Everyone could soon return to hard research full time.

Somehow, he had come through again.

The House Call From Hell

(Adapted from *The Incubator*, by Mark R.
Sneller, in Strange Adventures,
Ghost River Images, Publ. 2021)

With rare exceptions, Jeff had given up making house calls, although an occasional caller might entice him to do so as a favor. He didn't need more angst after his recent adventures. Money had nothing to do with it. At least his short-lived project coordinating with Chatfield Pharma on the orange mold gave him a chance to stretch him mind. He thought something as basic as a house call would be a refreshing change, like going home to see mama.

He certainly didn't need what happened next, when he went on the house call from hell.

I refuse to die with freaking black bread mold growing on my skin and inside me in a humidity chamber, as if I were a loaf of bread in a sealed package.

Four of us were holed up in a home on the outskirts of Lawton, Oklahoma, about an hour's drive from Oklahoma City, southwest along U.S. Highway 44, and slightly less if you're coming from the University of Oklahoma in Norman. Let's keep it simple: A very unpleasant death appeared to be the singular option because of its utter grossness.

We were entombed in a life-sized culture dish, or, death-sized, if you will, solidly trapped in a warm room with mold growing at our feet which began to grow on and in our bodies. Only one uncertainty remained: the manner of our death: Would it be a slow respiratory strangulation or would it occur by some unknown and probably hitherto undescribed affliction?

A cloudless sky greeted me in the cool morning air as I left Norman and drove to Lawton. I had received directions from the insurance company on how to find the new neighborhood because it would not yet be listed to make my GPS functional. I took in the upscale residences in the neighborhood and the quality of the late model vehicles parked in the drives. No cars up on blocks around here. A number of lots were vacant and several had houses under various stages of construction. The housing business appeared to be good shape in north Lawton.

The Thomas' residence stood at the end of a cul-de-sac in a quiet neighborhood on a rise with a view of a small lake to the south. A similar style home stood next to it to the west. Vacant lots occupied the remaining portion of the immediate area with dogwood and elm trees predominating the local vegetation. An occasional towering pine made its point.

Pulling into the large drive with my SUV, I parked behind one of two pickup trucks already parked there, one of them a clean white Ford 150. Lettering on the door read: "Ted's A/C and Heating, Lawton OK," with a phone number beneath the lettering. I looked upward and saw two men on the roof working on the air conditioning units. Presumably the units belonged to the upper and the lower portions of the home. Music blared from a small radio near where the men worked.

I parked behind the second truck, a beat-up old Toyota with some dents on the driver's side. The rear bumper had been displaced. On the door were the words "Ken's Restorations—We serve all of Oklahoma," painted in red. Smaller letters presented a phone number.

I moaned. From riches to rags. From cheery sunlight to darkness in a flash. Please, not Ken. *Jeff, bail out or enter the twilight zone.*

Indeed, to reinforce my bad decision to see what could go wrong, to ensure Murphy's Law had not vacated the premises, my old nemesis, Mister Crew Cut Ken Bradley, stepped out of his truck to greet me. Apparently, the insurance company had made a terrible mistake and hired Ken's Restorations to conduct the repairs. Notice I didn't say, "Complete the repairs."

"Junk people drive junk cars," somebody had

once told me. While that didn't apply to most professional people with whom I associated, in Ken's case, it couldn't be a truer statement, although the word 'professional' might be stretch.

Nose-and-Tongue Ring Ronnie, his six-month-pregnant well-tattooed bimbo assistant stepped out of the passenger side wearing cutoffs and sneakers. Her pink butch haircut added a perk to her dress ensemble.

I suspected Ken had already trained Ronnie in other matters. No doubt his former wives would agree. Word had it he was three times divorced and made child support payments for five children. The expenses were killing him. After the first two, he swore off women and got married again with the understanding there would be no babies. His latest divorcee assured him she was fixed and there was no way she would have any children. She had triplets. Couldn't have happened to a more upstanding citizen. Now Ronnie had entered the picture.

She was not without her own issues. She'd moved from company to company because of a modest background in her father's construction business. Ronnie got fired each time for various violations related to "consorting issues." Obviously, Ken's Restoration found that she possessed the necessary skills to be an important adjunct to his business. This suggested she'd worked for him several months, given the state of her pregnancy.

When the call came to my office, the insurance company told Carmen that the homeowners, Thomas by name, would be gone for the day. Both wife and husband were attorneys. She worked in Lawton. He worked in Oklahoma City. Carmen told me to get the key from the man next door to the south. We scheduled the time that I would inspect the area that had the problem. Nobody told me Mister Wonderful would be there.

In this particular case, a water supply line to the upstairs bath had broken thanks to city pressure testing. A retired neighbor who watched homes for the neighborhood had discovered the water loss soon after it occurred and had called a plumber to prevent further damage after checking with one of the Thomas's. The city wasn't talking about when the pressure testing occurred. It never does.

I can formulate a number of reasons why we do things against our better judgment. These reasons might include desire to please, desire for a better outcome than the first or second time, bucking heads with fate because you were in the mood to do so, a poor perspective on the problem at hand, and so forth.

Therefore, despite my better judgment based on hard lessons, common sense, and a screaming voice in my head to run away, I agreed to permit both Ken and Ronnie to accompany me, and thusly, had permitted bad luck to be my partner for the job. In a word, it all falls on my head.

Neither of us even thought about shaking hands when we met that day. Our shared experiences go back years when somebody had to fix his messes.

My feeble mind could not fathom why he still remained in business.

As if he had been called by name, the neighbor came out of his house with the key and introduced himself as Walter Fitzgerald. Walter appeared to be somewhere in his seventies with most of his faculties. Everybody in the neighborhood relied on him to look after their home in their absence, according to him. Walter shook hands with Ken and said, "Say, we met a few days ago. Right? You too," he said to Ronnie.

"She was here with you?" I asked Ken.

"She needs the experience," he replied.

Walter and I shook hands. The top two buttons of his shirt were undone and I could see a lengthy well-healed scar beginning from the top of the breast bone and dropping down beyond sight; a sure indication of open heart surgery.

Walter led us to the front door, inserted the key and bade us enter the domicile. "Can I see what you've done so far?" he asked to nobody in particular.

"Sorry, Walter, we don't like non-work personnel to enter a contained area."

"Oh, it isn't contained," responded Ken. "We didn't need to."

"Then I can go in," Walter said, enthusiastically.

"Sure," responded Ken.

"No, you can't," I stated flatly. "It's against regulations and common sense."

Walter looked at Ken who just shrugged. If that was an emotion from Ken, it might be the first one ever observed. Walter waited an instant and saw that I remained resolute, so he returned to his house. The three of us entered through the unlocked front door and Ken led us up about fifteen steps to a balcony area with a railing that overlooked the great room. The homeowners had good taste in artwork and furnishings.

Ken led us down the hall to the bathroom at the end of the hall on the right. The door was only partially closed, nor contained in heavy-gauge plastic, and wasn't taped shut. An air return register was set in the ceiling outside the bathroom.

Before the bath, we passed one bedroom and across the hall lay two more. Ken told me his company had removed the upper layer of flooring from the water damage and needed an inspection and clearance test to check for the presence of mold. I was reluctant to permit a pregnant woman to be on-site under conditions where the unknown prevailed, but Ken assured me we would be in and out of the bad area within only a few short minutes. Also, he wanted her to gain more experience.

Ken pushed on the swollen oak door and it refused to be moved. He placed his right shoulder against the door and pushed. The door opened, albeit reluctantly. "Tell you what," he said, proudly, "What's inside sure stays inside."

I entered the room and hauled along a collapsible tripod, a cosmetic case containing air pump, collection cassettes, and other accouterments necessary for air and surface testing. Ronnie and

Ken followed me. As I opened my mouth to caution him, Ken leaned his hulking shoulder against the door and slammed it shut.

Once inside, I flipped on the light switch and five one-hundred watt bulbs were reflected off the vanity mirror. The simple bathroom held a single-sink vanity and a step-in shower; no tub. I could see the shower surround consisted of a single piece of wrap-around plastic. A small window above the window brought sunlight into the room. *Pretty cheap for a custom built home,* I thought. At the same time I saw that the floor was completely black. Taking it for glue-down mastic, I asked Ken about it because the place reeked terribly with eye and throat-burning pungency. "There is no mastic. This is just the layer between the upper and lower portion of the sub-flooring. We cut the floor in a jiffy and that was that," he retorted matter-of-factually.

Wrong. My mental alarm bells went off and I immediately took out a quick sticky tape surface sampler and touched it to the black floor we were standing on. My portable microscope didn't lie and neither did my nose. This could only bespeak of formaldehyde, octanol, along with a score of petrochemicals produced by actively growing mold.

Looking up from the microscope, I provided the male portion of my audience with the bad news trying to hide the quaver in my voice, yet smiling all the while. Trust me, the smile was born out of great fear. "Did the thought ever cross your mind that whatever you do, you do it wrong? We are standing on what looks like a pure culture of *Aspergillus niger*. This mold loves to grow on damp structural materials. To the human, it is invasive and does very nicely in persons with a lowered immune response, such as guys like you."

Ronnie looked frightened. Holding her belly, she asked, "Is that as bad as the black mold?"

"It is black," interjected the gym rat, proudly exhibiting his vast knowledge about colors. "That makes it black mold."

It's worse than that, folks. My armpits were beginning to sweat. I said, "No, actually this is the same kind that grows inside your bag of bread." This particular species produced ten thousand times the number of spores than did the reputed famous black mold known as *Stachybotrys*. "Just about any microbe can be harmful under the right circumstances. We have the perfect circumstances right here. You locked the three of us in a trap, Ken. If it grows on wood and petroleum-based glue-downs and bread, and fruit and dust, and soil, why the hell shouldn't it grow on a person's flimsy body?"

I hadn't meant to be so gruff, but Ken is one of those people who knows how to push your buttons. Under these circumstances, as the expert in the room, I had no reason to skirt the issue. Everybody needed to know the facts. "Why do you think your eyes are burning?" I threw in as a closer.

"My eyes aren't burning," Ken responded.

"Those must be tears of joy," I commented. "I estimate the level of toxic gases is a good hundred times the normal indoor concentration. Face it, if the spores don't get you, the poisons in the air will."

"Then we need to get out of here," Ronnie screeched.

"Exactly," I commented.

"Okay, let's go," shrugged Ken, as easily as if he were pumping another set of barbells—dumbbells in his case—and probably wondering what all the fuss was about. He made a move to grab the door handle.

I knew he would try that and said, "In case you didn't notice, the upstairs air return register is located in the hallway just outside this bathroom, in the 'OFF' cycle when we came in. Now it's 'ON', and if we open the door, the register will suck in spores from this room and send them into every room. Then the home will have to be cleaned."

"The filter will take care of that," contributed Ken, smartly, digging deep into his vast warehouse of memorized facts. I wanted to slap him. "And don't talk to me what to do or what to notice," he concluded.

"Somebody has to since your mother isn't here." I tried to push the bastard to the limit, adding, "Were you born stupid or did you take advanced classes?"

My mouth owned me, not the other way around. "First, why didn't you get this vanity out of here? The commode, as well. You damn well know the mold is going to grow on the particle board of the counter and grow beneath the unit.

"Number two: The filters that are here will not handle spores this small. Basically, whatever is harmful goes in one side of the filter and goes out the other side."

"You're just full of knowledge, doctor. It must be nice to have a career where you get to run people down." We were both seated and were facing eye-to-eye.

"That wasn't the bad news, bubba. That was the good news. The bad shit will come later," I whispered, such that only he could hear it. "You know, when the mold begins to grow out of your nose and mouth. And you made it all happen. Lucky us."

Which probably won't happen until after we were all dead, but I didn't feel like telling him that part. Let the prick think about it.

"I have to pee," whined Ronnie.

"Tie it in a knot," sneered Ken.

I so dearly wanted to throw down with the guy. The kid might be promiscuous, but she had to deal with her pregnancy while stuck in this bathroom with the two of us arguing.

The man stood six-two and weighed two-thirty. He carried too much belly fat, but one couldn't deny he possessed a lot of arm and shoulder strength. He'd been a bully all his life. The time had come for the bullying and life as he knew it to come to an end. As things stood, it could also apply to all of us. (Thankfully, Walter had not been trapped in this room with us when Ken had slammed the door shut. The nightmare could have been a screaming death for all of us.)

In contrast, I stood five-eleven, weighed fifty pounds less and ran a lot. My old college years as a water polo player and karate guy gave me endless memories of the old days. Today, my temperament and drive remain to motivate me every single day.

Ken and I were both in our early forties. I could still hit as hard as ever whenever the seductive temptress of opportunity smiled my way. This temptress was giving me a side-wise, yet encouraging glance, which bespoke the words: "Just a straight shot to the point of the chin." I shoved out further thoughts best left unspoken.

Instead, I put my actions into words. If you can't strike while the iron is hot, use a different hot iron. Besides, a good fighting philosophy is this: If you defeat your opponent physically, he can come back to hurt you. If you defeat him in spirit, the victory is permanent. If you defeat him physically and in spirit, it's a fair guess you won the battle.

I said, "Shut up, Ken. You're the one who didn't fix this place properly. You didn't set up a proper dehumidifier; you didn't set up proper protection outside this room. And what were you thinking when you removed the top flooring? You knew there would be water retention between the layers of particle board. Boy, are you a royal screw up."

I began to disturb myself. I had become unscientific and too pissed off. Okay, it felt good to become belligerent with this monkey, although that didn't help the cause of self-preservation, especially because the path down the future road frightened the hell out of me. Literally rotting away in a jail cell for hurting this guy held no attraction to me. Neither did trading my life for his. I'd rather rot away in the comfort of my own home with a bottle of quality Russian vodka in my hand than be comfortably ensconced in a jail cell.

My immediate problem had become Ken, as if he were an object, an end goal. On second thought, my immediate problem had become my thinking process. Habitually, I face a problem head-on, not avoid it. For some reason, I feel secure doing that. Let the shrinks work that out. I found myself out of character, deflecting, not trying to solve the problem of escape. Instead, I made Ken into the problem, which made absolutely no sense unless my thinking process was becoming warped. Only one thing could explain that.

Ken knew I had hurt him when I brought up his job performance, but the humanoid said nothing. No great surprise, because one of his many nicknames is "Ken—my dick is bigger than your dick—Bradley." Normally he would have a retort whenever somebody espoused real knowledge and he'd try to modify your knowledge based on the narrow range of his own life experiences.

I couldn't stop my mouth. If my previous comments didn't hit him in the BBs, maybe the next salvo would do it. My thoughts carried me to the extreme. I teetered between rage and professional behavior, legal versus wanton destruction of another human, yet not concentrating on finding a way out of this mess. My throat was getting sore from the chemicals in the air and from talking so much in this alien environment.

I almost shouted, "Not only that, Ken, but you screwed up the big hospital job last month. You allowed the containment barrier to fall down and you exposed the cancer patients to a high concentration of mold spores that killed two people. Oh, I'm sorry, didn't you follow the cases? I had access to the autopsy reports."

"Hey, don't tell me how to do my job. I've been doing this stuff since I turned fifteen," Ken puffed himself up. "How long have you been lording it everybody you meet? I mean, when the word got out you would be on this job, I just tingled with excitement."

"Oh, you got me there, Ken. My parents made me go to school so I could learn to read and write and add and maybe gain a few social skills. So you've been unprofessional a lot longer than I've been professional. Don't you even care that the same mold spores I identified were the same ones that killed three people?"

"Bullshit, Shenero. They were dying anyway. And nobody can prove your mold killed them."

My mold? "Wrong again, Bradley. Watch for the coroner's report and make plans for another life. It's called either second or third degree murder. Probably second because your negligence caused the deaths."

Ronnie jumped on the band wagon. "Yeah, Bradley. You're a screw up. That's all you ever do, isn't it? Screw things, up!" Her hands flew to her belly. Another rumor had it that Ronnie always called men by their last name, even in bed.

"Hey," Ken responded defensively, almost flippantly, as the great ape postured. "I hired a bad worker. It can happen to anyone."

"No matter what, you're responsible and you're the bad worker," inserted Ronnie. "I was there. Remember? You told me a whole different story from what the doc here says and I believe him. So, you think this is bad, wait until we get into court. We'll see what I can get for child support. You lied to me, Bradley."

Gee, Ronnie, why beat around the bush? And what did he lie to her about? Did he say he loved her or perhaps make her a partner or he would give her money or take care of the baby? Knowing Ken, my guess is that he dug himself a hole in which he is presently standing and is proceeding to pull in the dirt behind himself.

The man stared at me as though he had been watching TV for twelve hours straight. But the sub-human refused to give up the fight. From nowhere he brought forth a bellow: "Sure, Ronnie, you've got two others you're collecting free money on. What's one more?"

"Back at you," she volleyed, spittle flying from her lips.

Ronnie began to rub her temples. I felt the same way. It wasn't like smelling a little musty dirt. Here, the odors would soon go away, an indication the chemicals were deadening the sense of smell—a defense mechanism. It could happen with perfume and it could happen with poison. Our brains would want for oxygen thanks to bad chemicals dissolved in the blood. Our thinking would cloud and things could go very bad after that. Correction: Our thinking is already clouded.

True as all this might be for the sake of science, we were trapped in a damned bathroom with no obvious way out. "All right, guys. How about we hop onto the vanity so we don't disturb the spores on the floor," I said, doing an about face from my thoughts and deflecting the conversation back to the problem at hand, a good deflection from endless accusation. Generally I use people like Ken as a measuring stick. If one does exactly the opposite of what they suggest, you're bound to be right almost all the time. If the idea had come from him I might have thought there would be something wrong with it and would be tempted to stay put.

Parts of the floor puffed up with spores as we moved. Other parts were so wet and slimy that we chanced slipping and falling, if we weren't careful. I knew we were already covered with the tiny life forms and once on the skin or on clothing, each of the millions and billions of tiny three micron-size spores would be sending forth a germ tube, just like a bean projecting a sprout in order to begin growth into an adult. They will quickly mature into another plant with countless seeds of its own. With one major difference: Beans didn't digest fabric, flesh, lungs or brain tissue. If you get enough bad guys overrunning the stockade, your defenses won't matter anymore.

My progressively worsening thought sequences drove me to cold sweats. Dying didn't bother me. Dying under these circumstances along with these two scared the hell out of me. What would we do when the end came? Would we hold hands and sing or forgive each his own trespasses?

I gently hopped onto the vanity, with Big Ken next to the door, me sitting in the middle and Ronnie sitting on the far edge with her feet resting on the commode and her back to me. The shower was directly in front of her. Where I sat, the faucet poked me in the back. I had about three inches on the edge to work with.

"What other complaints do you have," Ken sniped with considerable venom. His day-to-day mood swings were well known, but today under pressure, the man appeared to be on the fringe of being out of control. We all were.

Ronnie attacked, pivoting around so she faced the same direction as we were and looked sharply to her left so she could eye Ken. "Complaints, Ken? How about the fact that you should be cleaning toilets for a living, You'd probably screw that up too. Here's the drama. Yes, the baby is yours and I'll prove it when the time comes. That'll be when I file a lawsuit against you for this mess right here."

Unless I miss my guess, Ronnie had decided she didn't like her latest employer. The woman was sharp and must have had some kind of education. I liked the part about the lawsuit. That meant I would get to testify in detail about Ken's incompetence. If I lived through this.

If Ken felt dejected, he didn't show it. Instead, he wouldn't let it go. "What's the matter, Ronnie? Don't you love me anymore? You sure loved me once."

"Does drunk and nearly asleep your definition of love? Do you remember when I said, 'No'?"

Ken laughed. "You saying 'no'? That's a laugh." The man ran a hand through his crew cut—a nervous reaction.

"Okay, little man. You give your version to the judge, and the baby and I will give ours," she sneered.

Good point, Ronnie.

Ken shrugged. Nothing affected this guy.

Suddenly, the power went off. In true Einsteinian fashion, a physicist might say there occurred a folding back of the space-time continuum where two disparate crises meet at the same time and in the same place. Others like me might say, "Oh, shit, what now?"

The power outage had undoubtedly occurred because the workmen were servicing the air handlers on the roof. We weren't in total blackness because a small window above the shower permitted a little of the early morning light to enter the room, albeit the window faced the north.

"This is good," said Ken. "There is no suction outside from the air return to spread the spores through the house so we can get out of here."

"You mean like you probably did the first time you worked on this room? Go for it," I suggested, knowing what would happen; actually awaiting the outcome of his antics in a diabolical manner, expecting comedy relief.

From his seated position on the vanity next to the door, Ken pulled on the door handle, silently at first, then followed by entertaining noises. The brute grunted and stained as hard as he could. The door had swollen into place, as if had been welded to the door frame, thanks to Ken's initial shove against the entire door to slam it shut. His meager efforts were a cheap comedy show, with only our lives on the line.

Ronnie and I did an eyeball exchange which triggered a laughing attack that only stopped when we both began to cough and gag from the spores and the stink in our lungs. Every time either of us began to talk the laughter began anew. Finally, with a hoarse and raspy voice, I managed to utter, "Uh, Ronnie, I wonder how the door got closed so tightly."

Through her own tears, Ronnie directed her attention to her former bed partner. "Now what, big shot?"

The employee had just fired the employer. The woman did have her little peccadilloes, like having unprotected sex and not learning from her mistakes. Like everybody, she had her own hornet's nest to deal with. But she had a wit and might have turned out all right in another life. Who knows, she might, yet. Before Ken could give a rejoinder, she added with a plaintiff cry, "I really have to pee."

"Go ahead and use the shower drain, if you need to," I said. "We won't watch." At least Ronnie had a door to close to cover her actions.

If Ken had spoken a single word during these moments, my right fist would have spoken for me, but we didn't need a writhing bleeding body on the ground to cause the release of more spores. Hopefully, my time with Ken would come, just him and me—no witnesses.

Shifting from my uncomfortable position, I stretched out my legs. I felt as though I sat on one of those old fashioned stocks to sit in public for days on a wooden board with a thin ledge going across your ass with your arms bound onto some other device. The only thing missing here was people throwing stones or rotten fruit at you.

So far, we had accomplished nothing. The jerk continued being a jerk; he and I were coming to blows, Ronnie had to pee, and there nobody had any creative thinking. So be it. Would it be necessary to tell them what will happen if we don't get out? It's coming to that.

What were the spores doing on my skin? That was the first thing I had to know, like a bubble forming way beneath the surface to finally rise atop the muck.

My work equipment lay in the bag at my feet, so I hooked one of the straps on my nylon tote bag with my foot and pulled up the bag to where I could reach inside. In the dim light, I pulled the portable microscope from its small case that measured about five inches on each side. I retrieved a microscope slide from the bag and scraped my exposed arm skin with one edge and along my face with another edge, followed this with the placement of a cover slip over the cells that I had scraped off. I placed the slide beneath the self-lighting scope to witness a quite spectacular view.

Countless small black spherical spores were sending down tiny germ tubes into my skin. These would soon become threads of mycelium. The cold sweat of fear ran from my forehead down the back of my spine and mingled with the stench of the petrochemicals in the humid air. I repacked the instrument and set the bag back down on the floor.

Her own task completed, Ronnie returned to her perch and offered, "An idea," she held up one finger. "How about if we all fit into the shower. Can't we wash this stuff off of us?"

"Theoretically . . ." I began to explain the plusses and minuses of her suggestion, until Ken chimed in.

"It won't work," he said. "Before we cut out the sub-floor, I turned off the water to both floors at the manifold in the utility room."

Ronnie began to cough and scratch her neck.

Somebody once thanked me for giving them moral support for their project. In Ken's case it would be safe to call it immoral support. I don't know how it works. All I know is that whatever some people touch or try to do turns out wrong almost all the time. Is it tied to the thinking process or something below that; some, as yet, undefined truth to the universe?

This bastard needed a "real larnin'," as country folk like to say. If we survive this, I'll take care of Ken, trust me on that. I'm like a dog latched on to a pants cuff. Except for one minor addition: I go for the jugular. This guy had a bad reputation. He paid off plumbers to obtain referral on water-damaged buildings, strictly against industry policy. He gouged the homeowners whenever he or his small staff of employees did the work. Since the insurance industry paid him directly, Ken felt he could charge whatever he wanted. So far, he'd gotten away with it. However, if I should survive this day, Ken will become my new pet project. He had no business in this business. How many times I didn't know about had he endangered the lives of others? How many people had actually gotten ill or died as a result of his incompetence?

Why was I so flagrantly hostile to this man? Incompetent people are a dime a dozen. Is it because of the many lives he has negatively affected? Maybe because people like him give the industry a bad name? No, that's too thin. Perhaps there existed some underlying factor where I saw myself in him, in some regards? There must be a psychiatrist somewhere who would be willing to put the blame on me because of my intense distrust and dislike of another person. The shrink might say, "What the hell's the manner with you, Shenero? How dare you dislike a man who tries so hard to make an honest dollar and raise a family? Or two? Or three?

No. Ken exuded the quality of dislike from the

first day we'd met years before. If he had any positive qualities they were well hidden. You could look into his eyes and they were always the same: stone cold, humorless, emotionless—a shell filled with a cluster of mistakes and bad luck events waiting to happen. The bells were ringing to toll our deaths together. Hopefully, it would be in mortal combat. Guaranteed it would not be in loving embrace.

I shook my head. The chemicals were taking over. The violence could start with me.

Ronnie sat next to the role of toilet paper, so I asked her to tear off several squares for us to hold over our mouths and noses to breathe through. I didn't want to give one to Ken. I wanted him to breathe in the spores and become a case study for the medical literature. But I did anyway. At least the paper would keep out the spores, but not smell of chemicals. The bathroom stunk like a toxic waste dump. In fact, by the EPA's definition, this room actually did qualify as an undesignated storage facility for toxic and hazardous substances. Certainly, the formaldehyde produced by the mold was at least equal to the amount found in any new manufactured home. At least builders are required to post a warning about the issue. How many homes provided to the New Orleans' Katrina disaster victims were unsuitable for habitation just because of one problem alone? Tears ran from my burning eyes. I tried not to look at the floor; black in its entirety.

"Doctor Shenero, maybe you could bang on the ceiling with your tripod and somebody could hear us," Ronnie offered, with limited enthusiasm.

Ken scoffed at the idea, but I tried it for several minutes to no avail. Apparently the pounding did not overcome the music coming from a radio on the roof.

"Here's another idea," I said, and pulled out my cell. "Ken, we're going to call your company and instruct them to set up a critical containment barrier outside this room with a change of clothing for all of us including themselves and for them to force the door open with whatever means so we can get out."

Four people's lives were at stake here including the baby and all were in the hands of Ken. Scary thought. His motto should be: *If you can't do it wrong, then don't do it at all.* For years, I'd taught this stuff at the university and now I was here; hopefully not making history.

"It'll take them two hours to get here to do all that," Ken said, his voice objective.

"You on a schedule?" I queried, noting that Ken stood a good chance of being the most likely to be the first to be infected thanks to his poor immune response, in turn thanks to his steroid usage. I got Ken's office number from him since it is not part of my Contact's list, hit SPEAKER, and punched in the number. NO SERVICE appeared on the screen.

"Let's try yours," I demanded, rather than suggested.

Resignedly, he gave it to me and I got the same response. "I could have told you there is no service out here," Ken contributed, smugly. I should have guessed. A nasty storm came through here the previous week and had probably taken out the cell phone towers.

I gently lowered myself from the counter and stepped into the shower stall. I tried the same number with each of the phones with the same non response. I tried 911 to no avail.

My mind's eye could picture the spores beginning to grow in our lungs and black fuzzy mold covering all of our bodies while being poisoned by the mold's chemical byproducts. I saw newspaper headlines: *Trio found dead in bathroom covered with black masses of mold. Workers gag and several hospitalized. Experts fear the contagion may spread. Lawton Health Department calls CDC to investigate.*

I began to scratch and cough. The itching that Ronnie exhibited had become real for both me and Ken. We also scratched various exposed places on our body and coughed. I desperately wanted to relate to him in lurid detail about how we were lower on the food chain than the spores which were utilizing our bodies as substrates for their survival and, concomitantly, for our demise. If Ronnie had been absent, no problem.

How long would it take for someone to figure out we were here? They couldn't reach us and we couldn't reach them.

"So what's going to happen to us?" Ronnie stared at me almost pleadingly, coughing as she spoke.

"We're all going to need medical attention. We're going to need to watch for symptoms of persistent coughing after we leave here and tell our doctor what happened. He might want to follow our lung function and run some blood tests."

Clinically speaking, of course. The last thing she needed to hear was the truth about mold growing inside her body and on her skin. Ken tried to give the appearance that he cared less about any of it. Hey, when you're a man, you're a man. Right Ken?

Ronnie declared. "Screw this and screw you both. I'm calling for help." She jumped down from the vanity to go for the window and hit a slick spot on the floor. She fell hard onto her back with one leg crumpled beneath her striking the vanity with her head. A dark cloud of mold spores billowed up from the floor as though someone had taken a fan to a quantity of gunpowder. The spores quickly melded with the rest of the air space and settled onto our bodies.

Ken looked on as if it were a TV commercial or a boring game show as I gently stepped down and slowly straightened her leg. Only semi-conscious, Ronnie cried out in anguish. I reached into my tote kit and pulled out a couple of small packets of alcohol wipes which I tore open and applied to an oozing area of blood on the back of her head.

Coughing, almost without control, I seated her onto the commode while she held her head in both hands. I said, "Look, how about if we just kick out a section of sheetrock between this room and the next. There's space between the commode and the vanity we can use. We'll tear out enough drywall to kick out the wall in the next room. Ronnie is the smallest one of us and can escape through the hole and go for help or make a call for help."

Seated on the vanity we faced the exterior wall and there would be no chance of escape through the shower. The door to the hallway was firmly swollen shut which left only one option.

"You better check for studs first," Ken advised.

I knocked on the wall between the commode and the vanity, a space of only fourteen inches. I hit a solid sound in the middle and hollow sounds on either side of that.

We all heard the vibrations and echoes and knew what they meant. I had hit a solid two-by-four wooden stud right in the middle. No escape there. Or could there be. Those studs are only attached at either end with nails. A few good kicks may do the trick to loosen at least one of them to aid in its removal. That was one plan. Were there any others?

"Okay, guys," I said, digging deep to sound confident. I felt as if we were on the right track. "Let's deal with the area above the commode. I can get up onto . . . "

"Forget it," contributed Ken. "That is, unless your pocket knife can cut through water pipes."

"No, but we can bang on them. I have a lot of metal objects in my kit. Even my knife will make noise."

"Not much. These are all plastic pipes," contributed Mister Positive.

I refused to die like a loaf of bread in a sealed

package. What would the headlines read after we were found and would my students say that Dr. Shenero died in the must perfect way for him.

My thoughts about my classroom took me to the stories I told about archaeologists who had found various tombs where mold grew on the mummies and who subsequently died because of the "curse of the mummy." They, too, had inhaled countless spores in a short period of time. Was this room to be our mummy's tomb?

"*What's inside sure stays inside*," Ken had said.

I muttered some curse words and began to cut out the sheetrock in the wall above and behind Ronnie, who sat bent over to make room for me, massaging her head with one hand and scratching various areas of her body with the other. She reminded me of a monkey.

The power came back on and our senses were blasted with a thousand watts of brightness just as our eyes were dark-adapting. Footsteps could be heard on the roof. The workmen were leaving. It also meant one man was already on the ground and had thrown the breaker switch and a moment later, their work truck started up.

"Ken, get to the window and yell for help," I demanded.

"Why me?" he asked.

"Because you're the dumbest one here and you're also the tallest and have the best chance of yelling through the window. That's why."

"What am I supposed to say?" asked Ken, in full

denial of the present circumstances.

"Hey, tell them you want to order a large pizza," Ronnie contributed, sarcastically.

The window faced the wrong direction anyway. There wasn't much chance for the men to hear anybody yell. They didn't. The truck drove off back to Lawton.

I had another idea. "Okay, big shot, let's see some of that steroid strength of yours. Grab the commode and rip it off the bolts holding it to the floor."

Ken saw I was serious when I took Ronnie by the arm led her into the shower to give him room to work. As if he does this sort of thing before breakfast every morning, the beast wrapped one arm around the tank and one around the base of the commode he began to yank and pull and rock it. Within sixty seconds the toilet lay on the floor and we had a good three-foot by five-foot hunk of drywall to work with. Ken and I started kicking. When we made holes, we grabbed the sheetrock and pulled it loose. We kicked out a couple of vertical studs and kicked out the adjoining wall in the adjacent bedroom. All three of us made it through the opening to freedom.

The entire home would not be expected to be contaminated because we had avoided opening the door to the bath and didn't have to expose the air return to the spores. A professional might request an entire air testing of the home for a variety of reason related to this event. That professional would be me.

I took my work equipment with me to the car sucking in deep breaths to try and clear my lungs. I went to the trunk, grabbed my gym bag, and walked back to utility room. I found the water control valves, turned on the one for the downstairs, left the one off for the upstairs, and took a long soapy shower in the master bath, coughing and blowing up as much muck as possible. I changed into my gym clothes, packed my khaki slacks, work shirt and shoes in the bag and returned it to the car. The other two were stood next to the truck a few feet away arguing heatedly. I checked my watch. It read almost eight thirty. Less than a half-hour had elapsed for the entire episode. So much for Ronnie's five minute exposure time.

I must have cut a great figure; a big yellow flower, standing there in sneakers, yellow jogging shorts and yellow Tee-shirt for visibility during street running. When I motioned for Ken to come over, he grinned and followed my beckoning wave like an obedient little doggie. I led him around the rear of the house, away from the prying eyes of Walter, as well as from Ronnie's view, should anybody ask her later about the incident.

A few moments later, I returned alone, gave Ronnie a slight wave, to which she gave me a Texas' Hook 'em Horns sign with her fingers. Then this bedraggled scientist climbed into his SUV and headed back to Norman.

Ken was going to have to deal with the insurance company that hired him along with their bills for damages he incurred regarding his negligence on this job, my formal report, lawsuits, various doctor's bills from my physician and Ronnie's, and his own.

He'd have to deal with the state health department, an assortment of lawyers including the homeowners' claims for damages, major dental surgery, and Ronnie.

I congratulated myself on making up the story about the deaths in the hospital. It might have happened, if the air currents hadn't carried the spores in the other direction. I figured the jerk would sweat plenty thinking about murder charges until it was time to sweat reality. I only hoped the reality wouldn't include illness or worse to Ronnie or me.

As it turned out, Ronnie and the baby were fine. It took her a couple of weeks for the cough to go away, but I have every faith she'll be healthy. I heard she moved in with her parents.

Not so, Ken. His cough got worse by the day. He didn't develop what we call Farmer's Lung from breathing in a lot of spores from mold growing on hay or grain. He developed a classic case of disseminated aspergillosis, in other words, with no immune system to control the little beasties, the spores spread throughout his entire body and his brain. He died a month later.

Sometimes mold spores do what they want. That the part will continue to bother me the rest of my life.

To the best of my recollection, that's how my dear husband told me the story, after which I massaged his neck and suggested to him he might want to go on a relaxing ocean cruise, this time to the Caribbean. It's not polite to tell you what he suggested to me. I'm sure he didn't mean it.

I am also certain that, once he gets back into his happy routine of research, he will be receptive to my reminder that it is time for us to start a family. It will be a simple loving request made at the appropriate time. What could go wrong?

About the Author

Mark Sneller, PhD, is a former professor of microbiology and medical mycology. He lives in Tucson, Arizona, where he operates Aero Allergen Research, a company specializing in indoor air quality and the identification of mold in contaminated buildings. He is the author of several health-related books, as well as the Jeffrey Shenero series of adventure novels.